MA

THE ST

MARGERY Sharp was born Clara Margery Melita Sharp in 1905 in Wiltshire. She spent some of her childhood in Malta, and on the family's return to England became a pupil at Streatham Hill High School.

She later studied at Bedford College, London, where she claimed her time was devoted 'almost entirely to journalism and campus activities.'

Still living in London, she began her writing career at the age of twenty-one, becoming a contributor of fiction and non-fiction to many of the most notable periodicals of the time in both Britain and America.

In 1938 she married Major Geoffrey Castle, an aeronautical engineer. On the outbreak of World War II, she served as a busy Army Education Lecturer, but continued her own writing both during and long after the conflict. Many of her stories for adults became the basis for Hollywood movie screenplays, in addition to the 'Miss Bianca' children's series, animated by Disney as *The Rescuers* in 1977.

Margery Sharp ultimately wrote 22 novels for adults (not 26, as is sometimes reported), as well as numerous stories and novellas (many of them published only in periodicals) and various works for children. She died in Suffolk in 1991, one year after her husband.

FICTION BY MARGERY SHARP

Novels

Rhododendron Pie (1930)*
Fanfare for Tin Trumpets (1932)*
The Flowering Thorn (1933)
Four Gardens (1935)*
The Nutmeg Tree (1937)
Harlequin House (1939)*
The Stone of Chastity (1940)*
Cluny Brown (1944)
Britannia Mews (1946)
The Foolish Gentlewoman (1948)*
Lise Lillywhite (1951)
The Gipsy in the Parlour (1954)
The Eye of Love (1957)
Something Light (1960)
Martha in Paris (1962)
Martha, Eric and George (1964)
The Sun in Scorpio (1965)
In Pious Memory (1967)
Rosa (1970)
The Innocents (1972)
The Faithful Servants (1975)
Summer Visits (1977)

* *published by Furrowed Middlebrow and Dean Street Press*

Selected Stories & Novellas

The Nymph and the Nobleman (1932)†
Sophy Cassmajor (1934)†
The Tigress on the Hearth (1955)†
The Lost Chapel Picnic and Other Stories (1973)

† *these three shorter works were compiled in the 1941 anthology* Three Companion Pieces

Children's Fiction

The Rescuers (1959)
Melisande (1960)
Miss Bianca (1962)
The Turret (1963)
Lost at the Fair (1965)
Miss Bianca in the Salt Mines (1966)
Miss Bianca in the Orient (1970)
Miss Bianca in the Antarctic (1971)
Miss Bianca and the Bridesmaid (1972)
The Children Next Door (1974)
The Magical Cockatoo (1974)
Bernard the Brave (1977)
Bernard Into Battle (1978)

MARGERY SHARP

THE STONE OF CHASTITY

With an introduction by
Elizabeth Crawford

DEAN STREET PRESS

A Furrowed Middlebrow Book
FM57

Published by Dean Street Press 2021

First published in 1940 by Collins

Cover by DSP

ISBN 978 1 913527 69 3

www.deanstreetpress.co.uk

To

GEOFFREY CASTLE

Introduction

'Miss Margery Sharp's witticisms lift the otherwise flat and unprofitable life of the village of Gillenham to the level of a bubbling champagne-glass full of laughter', wrote the *Sphere* reviewer (24 August 1940) of Margery Sharp's new novel, *The Stone of Chastity*. She had already been a professional novelist for ten years and over the course of a long career published a total of twenty-two novels for adults, thirteen stories for children, four plays, two mysteries, and numerous short stories.

Born with, as one interviewer testified, 'wit and a profound common sense', Clara Margery Melita Sharp (1905-1991) was the youngest of the three daughters of John Henry Sharp (1865-1953) and his wife, Clara Ellen (1866-1946). Both parents came from families of Sheffield artisans and romance had flourished, although it was only in 1890 that they married, after John Sharp had moved to London and passed the Civil Service entrance examination as a 2nd division clerk. The education he had received at Sheffield's Brunswick Wesleyan School had enabled him to prevail against the competition, which, for such a desirable position, was fierce. Margery's mother was by the age of 15 already working as a book-keeper, probably in her father's silversmithing workshop. By 1901 John Sharp was clerking in the War Office, perhaps in a department dealing with Britain's garrison in Malta, as this might explain why Margery was given the rather exotic third name of 'Melita' (the personification of Malta).

Malta became a reality for the Sharps when from 1912 to 1913 John was seconded to the island. His family accompanied him and while there Margery attended Sliema's Chiswick House High School, a recently founded 'establishment for

Protestant young ladies'. Over 50 years later she set part of her novel *Sun in Scorpio* (1965) in Malta, rejoicing in the Mediterranean sunlight which made everything sparkle, contrasting it with the dull suburb to which her characters returned., where 'everything dripped'. In due course the Sharps, too, arrived back in suburban London, to the Streatham house in which Margery's parents were to live for the rest of their lives.

From 1914 to 1923 Margery received a good academic education at Streatham Hill High School (now Streatham and Clapham High School) although family financial difficulties meant she was unable to proceed to university and instead worked for a year as a shorthand-typist in the City of London, 'with a firm that dealt with asphalt'. In a later interview (*Daily Independent*, 16 September 1937) she is quoted as saying, 'I never regretted that year in business as it gave me a contact with the world of affairs'. However, Margery had not given up hope of university and, with an improvement in the Sharps' financial position her former headmistress wrote to the principal of Bedford College, a woman-only college of the University of London, to promote her case, noting 'She has very marked literary ability and when she left school two years ago I was most anxious she should get the benefit of university training'. Margery eventually graduated in 1928 with an Honours degree in French, the subject chosen 'just because she liked going to France'. Indeed, no reader of Margery Sharp can fail to notice her Francophile tendency.

During her time at university Margery began publishing verses and short stories and after graduation was selected to join two other young women on a debating tour of American universities. As a reporter commented, 'Miss Sharp is apparently going to provide the light relief in the debates', quoting her as saying, 'I would rather tell a funny story than talk about statistics'. Articles she wrote from the US for the *Evening Standard* doubtless helped defray the expenses of the coming year, her first as a full-time author.

For on her return, living in an elegant flat at 25 Craven Road, Paddington, she began earning her living, writing numerous short stories for magazines, publishing a first novel in 1930, and soon becoming a favourite on both sides of the Atlantic. Her life took a somewhat novelettish turn in April 1938 when she was cited as the co-respondent in the divorce of Geoffrey Lloyd Castle, an aeronautical engineer and, later, author of two works of science fiction. At that time publicity such as this could have been harmful, and she was out of the country when the news broke. Later in the year she spent some months in New York where she and Geoffrey were married, with the actor Robert Morley and Blanche Gregory, Margery's US literary agent and lifelong friend, as witnesses.

During the Second World War, while Geoffrey was on active service, Margery worked in army education, while continuing to publish novels. *The Stone of Chastity*, which appeared at the time of the Battle of Britain, was described by the *Liverpool Evening Express* as a 'bucolic romp' that would 'defeat the black-out blues' (26 August 1940). The setting was Gillenham, an archetypal English village, 'old and backward for its age', the plot centring on the investigation by folklorist Professor Isaac Pounce into the 'old, Norse, and coarse' legend of the Stone of Chastity, a stone placed in the village brook which, if an unchaste woman stepped on it, caused her to stumble and fall. The author conjures up a cast of memorable characters drawn into this test of female virtue, so scientific that its methodology even includes a questionnaire. From her description,

Margery set Gillenham in the eastern part of the country and, although it may not have served as an exact model, was well acquainted with Tinwell in Rutland, home to her elder sister, with whom she often stayed.

In London Margery and Geoffrey lived in a set (B6) in the Albany on Piccadilly, where they were tended by a live-in housekeeper, and from the early 1950s also had a Suffolk home, Observatory Cottage, on Crag Path, Aldeburgh. The writer Ronald Blythe later reminisced, 'I would glance up at its little balcony late of an evening, and there she would be, elegant with her husband Major Castle and a glass of wine beside her, playing chess to the roar of the North Sea, framed in lamplight, secure in her publishers.'

Late in life Margery Sharp, while still producing adult novels, achieved success as a children's author, in 1977 receiving the accolade of the Disney treatment when several stories in her 'Miss Bianca' series became the basis of the film *The Rescuers*. She ended her days in Aldeburgh, dying on 14 March 1991, just a year after Geoffrey.

Elizabeth Crawford

CHAPTER 1

1

NOTHING could have been simpler, nothing more forthright, than the pattern made by the red roof of the Old Manor against the blue summer sky. To Nicholas Pounce, lying flat on his back in the garden, the ridge-poles of the main building and of the small jutting wing made a wide obtuse angle, cut only by the parallel verticals of the great chimney. Four lines, and two colours: primary blue, primary red. Nicholas stared so long that when he closed his eyes the pattern reappeared inside his lids, a silhouette, light on dark instead of dark on light; when he looked again the colours seemed to shout out of the sky, as though he heard them with his ear-drums as well as saw them with his eyes. Nothing could have been simpler, nothing more forthright; but beneath that simple, that forthright roof were some strange goings-on.

In the small gun-room, temporarily converted into a study, Professor Isaac Pounce was even then completing his questionnaire (later to be circulated through the unsuspecting village of Gillenham) on the subject of Chastity.

On the first floor Mrs. Pounce, mother to Nicholas and sister-in-law to the Professor, was lurking in her bedroom afraid to come out. She had appeared at lunch wearing a very nice necklace of scarabs and enamel, and the Professor, cocking an interested eye, had remarked that it was just such trifles—the sight of an English gentlewoman ornamented with seven phallic symbols—that made life so perennially interesting to the folklorist. Mrs. Pounce did not know what a phallic symbol was, and instinct (or possibly a look in her son's eye) prevented her asking; but after coffee she quietly sought out a dictionary and took it upstairs. At the moment she was feeling she could never come down again.

In the little room over the study Carmen was painting her toe-nails. No one knew much about her. She couldn't be the Professor's secretary, because Nicholas was that, and she couldn't be the housekeeper because the housekeeper was Mrs. Leatherwright. She was just there. She was there when all the Pounces arrived two days previously, and the Professor had evidently expected to see her, but had confined himself to the simple statement that This was Carmen. "Miss—?" enquired Mrs. Pounce gently. "Smith," said Carmen. But Nicholas at least had the odd feeling that she might equally well, and with equal truth, have said "Jones," or "Brown," or even "Princess Galitzine. . . ."

Nicholas thought a great deal about Carmen. He felt she would add greatly to the interest of his temporary internment in this remote pocket of the country. She seemed to be about twenty-eight years of age, which was six years older than himself, and he liked his women mature. He always had, and at Cambridge the taste had done much to establish his reputation as a sophisticate. "Pounce? He likes his women mature," his friends would say, doubtfully regarding their eighteen-year-old sisters up for the May Week balls; and though Nicholas, when pressed, would often allow himself to be thus partnered, it was always felt to be a concession. In point of fact his women to date numbered only two, both dancing-teachers, with whom his relations had been limited to rather half-hearted scufflings on divans, and it was for this reason that he had not joined the Oxford Group. He could not bring himself publicly to confess that his most poignant erotic memory was of a broken spring which twanged—oddly enough—on the note of B flat. The observation said much for his ear, but too little for his powers of concentration.

"Carmen," said Nicholas softly.

He willed her to come out of the house and kneel beside him, so that he could lie and look up at her tawny head against the sky. At that moment a door in the house opened. But it was not Carmen who came out. It was his Uncle Isaac, carrying the draft of the questionnaire.

2

The legend of the Stone of Chastity is old, Norse, and coarse. Its essential points may be gathered from stanzas in the naturalized ballads of *Willie o' Winsbury* (100 A, 4f) and *Young Beichen* (text A), and in these versions midwifery is quite plainly mingled with the magic: but the variant stumbled upon by Professor Pounce was purely supernatural. ("Stumbled upon" was the Professor's own phrase: in view of the facts, it pleased his academic sense of humour.) He stumbled upon it, then, in a manuscript journal, dated 1803, which he found in the attic of an East Anglian country-house while his hosts were looking for him to play bridge. After a slightly monotonous account of balls and toilets—the writer was evidently a very young woman—came an entry running thus:

Mr. C. back from Gillenham. I thank God in my striped India muslin, rose-colour sash. Mr. C. entertaining as ever; tells us of an odd strange legend, that in the stream there is a certain stepping-stone, on which if a Miss who should by rights have quitted that Title, or a wife unfaithful, set her foot, the poor creature infallibly stumbles and is muddied for all to see. 'Tis called the Stone of Chastity. Mamma shocked.

The sensations of the Professor on reading this passage are impossible to describe. He felt (he afterwards told his friend Professor Greer) a distinct prickling at the roots of his moustache, as though the individual hairs were erecting themselves one by one; but he carried no mirror, and this ancillary phenomenon had to go uninvestigated while he eagerly turned the journal's subsequent pages. Four days later the name of Mr. C. recurred:

Alone half an hour with Mr. C., Mamma being called to the preserve-boiling. I in my spotted India, black scarf. Mr. C. tells me that five months before his visit to G. a maidservant, a strapping fair wench by name Blodgett, or Blodger, challenged by her mistress to make trial of the S. of C., did so out of brazenness in her Sunday print, white stockings, fine black shoes, green garters. All ruined by the stinking mud. She now the mother of a fine boy. Mamma returned, I read aloud a passage from Cowper.

Feverishly Professor Pounce fluttered the leaves, but found nothing more of interest save one last reference to the entertaining Mr. C.—*"Mr. C. gone to-day, without visiting. The tradesmen much put out—"* Over this entry he paused some minutes; it seemed to cast a certain shaded light on the gentleman's character; but it did not, decided the Professor, in any way discredit his evidence. A carelessness in settling accounts could not affect his value as a witness. A graver fault was Mr. C.'s obvious desire to entertain; could he be trusted not to distort? Probably not; but here the Professor's specialized knowledge acted as a check. Casting his mind back to *Willie o' Winsbury* (100 A, 4f) and *Young Beichen* (text A) Professor Pounce decided that however embellished (as in the matter of green garters), Mr. C.'s tale was substantially reliable. That frivolous young man had happened upon a unique, an invaluable addition to the body of English folklore; by a fortunate chance he had passed it on to an equally frivolous young lady; through whom, by a chance more fortunate still, it had at last come into the right hands—the hands expert and incorruptible of Professor Isaac Pounce.

He determined to investigate at once.

Everything was propitious. The University term had just ended, the Long Vacation stretched gloriously ahead. The idea of actual field-work, after years spent on texts, was positively intoxicating. The freshness of the evidence (only a hundred and thirty years old) filled him with hope. He did not quite imagine—delightful dream—that the ceremony of the Stone was still alive, that in the year 1938 suspected trollops, stockinged by Woolworth, were set up to prove their virtue on a relic of Norse legend; but he did expect hearsay evidence. If the Blodgett (or Blodger) line still existed, the girl's great-grandchild might be yet alive. . . .

In a beatific dream Professor Pounce slipped the journal into his pocket and came down from the attic. He did not mention his find to any one, because he knew how such things got about, and he wished to keep all the interest and credit of the investigation to himself until such time as he could astonish his colleagues with a monograph. But within twenty-four hours he had identified Gillenham on the county map, driven himself over, taken the empty Old Manor and acquired a housekeeper. The day after, he went back to London to fetch some clothes and shut up his Bloomsbury flat. (It must have been at this time that he sent down Carmen.) While packing he was called upon, to his great irritation, by his widowed sister-in-law and his nephew Nicholas. Mrs. Pounce, as usual, wanted to speak to him—she was always in difficulties with either her Income Tax or her landlord—and Nicholas was as usual unemployed. But he could type and spell (a degree in History, which Nicholas also possessed, represented in the Professor's eyes just so much wasted time), and he seemed not unintelligent. The Professor decided on the spot to take the pair of them to Gillenham. Nicholas could act as his secretary; there was plenty of room in the house for Mrs. Pounce to mope about. His impatience and irritation allowed no argument; the next day saw them en route.

Carmen must have made the journey alone.

3

"Nicholas!" said the Professor sharply.

Nicholas reluctantly sat up. Black patches danced before his eyes; the largest of them, steadying and expanding, resolved itself into the figure of his uncle. In person Professor Pounce was short, grey and wiry. He affected as a sort of academic undress a blue flannel jacket, double-breasted and brass-buttoned, which added to his appearance a faint smack of the sea. With the addition of a yachting cap he could have passed for a retired skipper, but he wore instead a neat panama with a black band. In one hand he carried a sheet of paper.

"Yes, sir?" said Nicholas, blinking.

"The questionnaire," said Professor Pounce. "I have finished it. I want you to type it out and deliver it to every house in the village. About fifty of 'em. You'd better get hold of a bicycle."

4

Obediently and eagerly—for it had not occurred to him that his uncle's procedure would be quite so businesslike—

Nicholas hauled himself to his feet and received the paper. The Professor's script was fallaciously neat and almost illegible, but a first glance assured Nicholas that the effort of deciphering would be amply repaid. The document ran thus:

Stone of Chastity—Questionnaire

Please complete and return to Professor Pounce, at the Old Manor.

Note.—Answer as many questions as you can, using one side of the paper only. Do not turn to Part II until you have completed Part I. All persons [the Professor had first written "candidates"] *are asked to sign their names at the end of the paper, and at the right-hand foot of the first sheet.*

PART I

α Have you ever heard of the Stone of Chastity? (Answer "Yes" or "No.")
β If "Yes," from whom?
γ When? (Date as accurate as possible.)
δ Was this evidence hearsay, or direct?
ε What was this evidence?

Now turn to Part II.

Nicholas eagerly turned. In Part I, he realized, his uncle had done his best to preserve a Gallup-like impartiality, to refrain from suggesting the required answer; Part II, Nicholas hoped, would be more expansive. It was.

PART II

It is very possible [began Professor Pounce affably] *that the legend of the Stone of Chastity has become distorted by time, and that it now exists, if at all, under another name. I will therefore recapitulate its main points:*

In a certain stream in or near Gillenham is or was a stepping-stone alleged to have the power of testing female chastity: i.e., *no unchaste virgin (presumed), no unfaithful wife, can keep her footing upon it, but stumbles into the water. The last test to be recorded was in 1803, when a Miss Blodgett, or Blodger, failed to pass. She is described as having worn a print dress, white stockings, black shoes and green garters; and later gave birth to a son.*

Please state whether this account, or any part of it, is already familiar to you; and/or whether you have heard of any other account showing any points of resemblance.

Note.—The evidence of any descendants of Miss Blodgett (or Blodger) will of course be particularly welcome.

5

"Well?" said the Professor impatiently.

Nicholas hesitated.

"Doesn't it cover the ground?"

"Completely," agreed Nicholas. "It's most comprehensive. But—"

"But what?"

"Doesn't it strike you, sir, that it might just possibly give offence?"

The Professor stared in honest amazement.

"Offence? How?"

"Well, this Blodgett-Blodger business, to begin with. Mentioning names. I mean, suppose anyone came to you and asked for evidence that your great-grandmamma was no better than she ought to be, mightn't you take it a bit—well—amiss?"

"Certainly not," replied the Professor. "Not if it were in the interests of science."

"Perhaps, sir, these people aren't scientifically minded."

"But what has that to do with me?" demanded Professor Pounce impatiently. "I can't make out what you're driving at."

Nicholas tried again.

"You don't think it may lead to trouble?"

"No, I do not!" cried the Professor, now thoroughly exasperated. "What trouble? What kind of trouble?"

"Well, sir, we've got to live here, at any rate for a time, and if the village people cut up nasty it may be a bit unpleasant. People don't always care to answer questions."

"They do. That's exactly the point brought out by these American polls. People *like* answering questions."

"But not about the chastity of their great-grandmothers."

Professor Pounce groaned aloud.

"You're as bad as your mother," he said. "Argue, argue, chatter, chatter, and never a word of sense. I shall expect that typing to be done by to-night—and don't use more than two carbons."

Obediently, but less eagerly, Nicholas carried the manuscript indoors.

6

So far, the village and the Manor had not met. So far, the Pounces, and even Carmen, were no more than mere summer visitors, economically welcome, personally negligible. So far, so good.

In the old gun-room, now a study, Nicholas uncovered his typewriter.

Chapter 2

1

No sound of his typing reached the village: the Old Manor was separated from it by half a mile of tangled lanes. By how much further, as now inhabited, was it separated in thought, in outlook, in moral and intellectual culture? The village was old, and backward for its age. It had always been backward. Roman officers of the North African Horse, writing home to their Cornelias and Lavinias, mentioned it with disapprobation as a collection of pig-styes. The Angles and the Saxons contemptuously over-ran it. The Great Army of the Danes did not even bother to set it afire. A Norman captain gave it as a tip to one of his sergeants who had got him out of a jam. The sergeant disappeared after some trouble over a married woman, and Gillenham was quietly snaffled by one of William's Domesday-book surveyors, who built a house and illegally called it a Manor. After the surveyor rightly came to a bad end, his tenants pulled the place down and diverted its materials to their own uses. A Thirkettle built again on the foundations, after which the new house, still known as the Old Manor, passed from owner to owner until a firm of Ipswich solicitors let it to Professor Pounce.

None of these changes made much difference to the villagers, who went on cultivating their land, paying taxes when they had to, and as far as possible keeping out of harm's way. They were not a martial race: Queen Boadicea had given them their fill of fighting: between 710 and 1914 a Gillenham Roll of Honour could have shown only two names—John Uffley, who got his head broken in Kett's rebellion, and John Fox, who, visiting that town on business, took an involuntary part in the Siege of Colchester.

The centuries passed, and Gillenham was still backward. There was no Great House to spread the light of civilization. The wool trade brought a small, evanescent prosperity. The energetic Mr. Coke of Norfolk slightly improved its methods of agriculture. The railways came, but did not come to Gillenham. Its insignificance may be judged from the fact that in 1938 there was only one public house, The Grapes. The other, and female, centre of communal life was the Village Hall, on which ground the Vicar's wife and Mrs. Pye waged a subterranean warfare for the leadership of the Women's Institute. Mrs. Pye's husband farmed the two thousand acres at Vander's, and was the most important man in the district. (The Cockbrows at Old Farm hardly counted, for they had been there only thirty years.) After Mr. Pye came Jim Powley, landlord of The Grapes, and after him the Vicar. Wives took the rank of their husbands. The fifty-odd cottages sheltered some three hundred lesser souls, mostly agricultural labourers living close to the soil without any apparent sense of the dignity of their lot. They were a plain tribe, sturdy but unhandsome; their talk was of bullocks, or occasionally, among the young ones, of film stars once seen and never forgotten. They addressed each other, man, woman and child, as "bor"; but this apparent indifference to sex was misleading—especially in spring.

2

Nicholas typed on. (Gillenham could not hear him.) To make fifty copies of a two-page questionnaire, using only two carbons, means typing thirty-four sheets in all; and he was very glad when, halfway through the fifteenth, sixteenth and seventeenth, he was interrupted by the appearance in the study door of Carmen Smith. She stood leaning against the jamb, nonchalantly buffing her nails, and let Nicholas look at her.

No one could have called her beautiful. Her face was too long, her features too large. Her tawny hair was rather coarse. She wore it cut in a thick straight bang across the forehead and drawn back behind the ears in a knot, after the style of a barmaid of the 'nineties. But her figure was remarkable—tall, very broad-shouldered, with proudly-jutting breasts, thin flanks, a small waist and long thighs. It wasn't a modern figure at all: it was too—Nicholas, finger suspended over the B of Blodger, sought painfully for an adjective—too crude. It reminded him of a Minoan figurine he had once seen at the British Museum. A Minoan barmaid, by Gum!

"Hello," said Carmen.

Nicholas grinned, and rattled off the next line at top speed, making three mistakes.

"You don't go very fast, do you?" said Carmen.

Nicholas grinned again without speaking. He had decided to be inscrutable. But the remark nettled him all the same.

"I know a girl who can do ninety," said Carmen.

Nicholas wished she wouldn't talk. A Minoan barmaid had no business to know girls who did typing. With the single-minded egoism of youth he already desired that Carmen should speak only the words, think only the thoughts, he considered appropriate to her.

"She makes four pounds a week," continued Carmen relentlessly. Her voice was low, but flat. "That's good money. Are you dumb?"

"No," said Nicholas. "I'm busy."

Carmen considered this with obvious scepticism. "You don't do much. At least, you haven't yet. I saw you in the garden all morning."

So she had been watching him from her window. Nicholas suddenly remembered the moment when he had sat up to scratch himself, and regretted it.

"Why didn't you come out and talk to me?" he asked.

"I was doing my nails." Carmen held up her left hand and regarded it steadily. It was bare, long-fingered, the nails coloured a deep petunia. Without shifting her gaze, she said, "Do you get paid?"

"No," said Nicholas. "Do you?"

"Of course."

The style of their conversation had been marked by no false delicacy.

"What for?" asked Nicholas.

Carmen continued to look at her finger-nails. Her thick dark eyebrows, perfectly straight, and paralleled by the line of her fringe, gave her gaze a peculiar intentness.

"Helping Mr. Pounce," she said; and moved nonchalantly from the doorway to let Mr. Pounce's sister-in-law come through.

3

Mrs. Pounce was determined to speak to someone. She had been sitting alone in her own room and feeling very unhappy. She didn't like being alone, and she didn't like the room. It wasn't a nice room at all. A nice room, in Mrs. Pounce's estimation, was one with a bright wallpaper, and a flowery carpet, and plenty of chintz, and a Benares brass tray or two. The room she was in had bare walls and a bare floor, and practically no furniture. Had she been a woman of action she could have gone to Ipswich and purchased at least the trays—for it is one of the advantages of Empire that Benares brass is readily procurable throughout the length and breadth of England; but a woman of action Mrs. Pounce was not. She was a talker, a gentle, persistent, harmless conversationalist; and it was indeed unkind of Fate to have cut her off from her sole and innocent activity. In a household of five persons (counting the daily girl) Mrs. Pounce had no one to speak to. Her brother-in-law was always too loud and impatient to let her get under way, her son seemed positively to avoid a *tête-à-tête*; she couldn't possibly speak to Carmen, and Mrs. Leatherwright, as soon as Mrs. Pounce appeared, had made a treaty with the Professor to the effect that no one was to be allowed in her kitchen. That left the daily girl, Joy, and though Joy was friendly enough she was kept too much on the run by Mrs. Leatherwright to have time for conversation.

So Mrs. Pounce had no one to speak to; and she could bear it no longer. She took off her nice scarab-and-enamel necklace, and locked it carefully away with a prophylactic hymn-book, and once more ventured out into the difficult world.

4

"Nicholas, dear," said Mrs. Pounce, closing the door behind her, "I want to speak to you."

Nicholas hammered rapidly at the keys.

"Stop making that noise, dear. I want—"

Nicholas stopped. He stopped, but his attitude was that of one expecting to go on again at any moment. This was no earthly good to Mrs. Pounce, who liked to settle to a conversation as to a game of bridge. It always took her a long time to get started, and what she had now to say was peculiarly difficult of approach.

"Well?" said Nicholas.

"Your father—" began Mrs. Pounce.

Nicholas fidgeted with his feet. Talk about his father always made him uncomfortable, for the late Ephraim Pounce had been, in a quiet way, perfect. His career as Branch Manager of the National and Shires Bank had been unblemished and useful, and at his untimely death it was discovered that every shilling of his small private income had been meticulously invested, year by year, in insurance and education policies for his wife and son. To do this, he had denied himself, as far as Nicholas could gather, every normal male pleasure, He neither smoked nor drank, nor would he play cards for money. His wardrobe was conservative and enduring—so enduring that a large portion of it descended to Nicholas, and embarrassed him very much. How such a sire could have produced such a son as Nicholas—Nicky Pounce of John's, who liked his women mature—was an eternal mystery, especially to Nicholas. He thought of his father with a sort of remorseful bewilderment: he was sorry the old chap had got so little fun out of life, yet could only suppose that the annual payment of insurance premiums had afforded some Puritan satisfaction. Nicholas sincerely hoped so; but the tale of his father's unremitting self-denial had been so drummed into him, for so many years, that he now disliked thinking about him at all.

"Your father—" began Mrs. Pounce again.

To his horror, Nicholas saw that her eyes were filled with tears. Pity and remorse—again remorse!—overwhelmed him. He disliked both emotions intensely, he loathed them, but he had a good heart. He got up and put his arm round his mother's shoulders and hugged her head clumsily against his chest.

"Darling," he said, "I know you think I've forgotten him. That I'm not grateful enough. But I haven't and I am. I know I'm not much of a credit to him, yet—"

He broke off, choked by natural honesty. The fact was he didn't want to be a credit to anybody. He wanted to be himself. And sometimes it seemed almost as though he couldn't be, simply because of that shining paternal example constantly dogging his heels. He knew that his father had wished him to enter the higher Civil Service; this Nicholas had refused to attempt, but the refusal left him with a permanent sense of guilt. He was still idling at an age when his father had already been six years at work; this too sometimes made him feel guilty—and sometimes defiant: he sometimes felt like being as idle as possible, just to even things up. All in all, the impeccable Ephraim Pounce had left his son an odd mixture of legacies.

"I don't talk about it much," said Nicholas desperately, "but I do honestly believe my father was the best man who ever lived."

No mother could have desired to hear more; Nicholas looked anxiously into Mrs. Pounce's face to see if she were comforted. But Mrs. Pounce had her eyes tightly shut, and tears still squeezed out under the lids. She shook her head gently from side to side; Nicholas held her more tightly, and again those disagreeable emotions filled his breast. He told himself he was ready to stand thus for hours. But after a few minutes he grew very tired of it.

"Darling," he said tentatively.

Mrs. Pounce sighed.

"I've got an awful lot of typing to do."

She sighed again.

"For Uncle Isaac. He's waiting for it."

"I wanted to speak to you," murmured Mrs. Pounce.

Nicholas restrained his impatience.

"All right, darling. I'm listening. What is it?"

"I can't, now," said Mrs. Pounce.

5

The Professor had stretched a cord across the lawn, over which he and Carmen were playing deck-tennis. The spectacle was curious: Professor Pounce, small but agile, leapt from side to side like a terrier in a pen, while Carmen, scarcely moving, stood close to the cord and shot out a long arm to the quoit. Her reach was terrific; in the most literal sense she was playing with the Professor. She never won a point by attack; she simply threw back the quoit, now left, now right, till the Professor was exhausted. A faint smile curved her lips; she looked almost benevolent. She looked indulgent, as a goddess might look in condescension to a mortal sport. For a moment Nicholas, as he came out of the house with his hands full of typescript, felt the full compulsion of her easy power; then he looked at the sweating, panting, ridiculous figure of his uncle, who was being made a fool of, and admiration was drowned in a flood of annoyance.

"Game!" gasped the Professor.

Nicholas put down the papers and walked on to his uncle's side of the court.

"Let me take her on," he said.

Across the cord Carmen stared at him thoughtfully. She was quite cool, not even her hair was ruffled. She weighed the quoit in her hand a moment, then tossed it from her.

"No, thanks," she said. "I've had enough."

Nicholas grinned maliciously. She thought he might beat her, and didn't care to risk it. For a second the notion gave him an absurd pleasure; then the expression on her face, of calm uninterest, as quickly destroyed it. He was by this time quite good at reading Carmen's expressions.

His uncle paid her. He didn't.

But what the deuce did his uncle pay her *for*?

CHAPTER 3

1

WOBBLING down the road next morning, on a borrowed bicycle with the bundle of questionnaires stacked in its carrier, Nicholas Pounce felt himself to be, both literally and figuratively, in a very precarious position. He was practically certain that only the front brake worked, and he was extremely apprehensive as to the effect upon its recipients of his Uncle Isaac's questionnaire. By a curious chance all the villagers he passed were able-bodied males. Some of them said "Mornin'" to him, and Nicholas said "Good morning" back. He said it ingratiatingly. In each stolid pair of eyes he detected, or thought he did, a complete lack of scientific interest and a fanatic regard for the good name of woman. Especially their own women. Rude chivalry. The questionnaires, in long blue envelopes, were conspicuous, and attracted notice in conjunction with Nicholas himself. The able-bodied males would all remember him as the young man who had taken them round. In a few days' time they would probably be looking for him with tar and feathers, and possibly a rail. The Professor wouldn't stop them, either. He liked to see old customs kept up.

A prey to these gloomy reflections, Nicholas reached the first outlying cottage. Its chief feature—indeed, the only feature he noticed—was a fine Staffordshire Bull-terrier. The Staffordshire Bull is still, though illegally, bred for fighting. Nicholas decided to call again on his way back. The next two dwellings were unguarded, and he was able to push an envelope under each of their doors. At the third, however, his approach had evidently been spied, for the door was opened, even as he stooped, by the lady of the house.

She was Mrs. Noah Uffley, and she looked a very powerful, uncompromising sort of woman.

"What's that?" demanded Mrs. Uffley.

"A—a letter," stammered Nicholas.

"Who from? What about?"

"Well, it's from my uncle—Professor Pounce," said Nicholas. "And it's about—it's about—er—magic, and so on."

To his surprise, her expression became more friendly.

"There was a Professor here last January," she remarked.

"Was there?" said Nicholas.

"Took the room behind The Grapes."

"Did he?" said Nicholas.

"He felt bumps," explained Mrs. Uffley. "On the head."

"Did he really?" said Nicholas,

"And played the trombone."

"You mustn't expect anything like that from Professor Pounce," said Nicholas, hurrying away.

This brief exchange, however, gave him an idea, and a very useful one: whenever questioned at subsequent doorways he simply said "Professor Pounce's Entertainment"—which in a way was not misleading, since he had no doubt that to some minds the Professor's questionnaire would prove very entertaining indeed. Moreover, it was by no means certain that the Professor could not feel bumps. Quite possibly he could also play the trombone; and Nicholas knew that his uncle would willingly exhibit both accomplishments in the interest of research. In any case, the casuistry lent him so much confidence that he rapidly disposed of forty-nine envelopes (placing the forty-ninth actually within the jaws of the Staffordshire Bull), and at last found himself on his way to the remotest dwelling of all—Rose Cottage, at the end of a bending lane; and here that confidence was his undoing, for it communicated itself to his legs. Nicholas pedalled rapidly—too rapidly—round the last corner, glimpsed another bicycle approaching, and the next instant discovered that he had been quite right about the brakes. Only the front one worked. Nicholas flew over the handlebars, knocked the oncoming machine sideways, and found himself sitting astonished in the dust opposite an equally astonished young woman.

2

"I say," said Nicholas, feeling his knees, "I'm frightfully sorry. I do hope you're not hurt. The fact is, I haven't been on a bicycle for years."

"I'm all right," said the young woman. "It's a beastly corner."

Her voice was pure Bloomsbury, the sort of voice which would have surprised Nicholas very much had he not been aware of the growing tendency among the intelligentsia to live in country cottages without sanitation. And as Nicholas recognized her voice, so did she evidently recognize his: they should really have met on the steps of the British Museum—or B.M.—but even in Gillenham their respective accents constituted an ample introduction.

"You've skinned your hand," said the girl. "You'd better come in and have some iodine on it."

Nicholas looked at his right hand, saw the blood oozing from a long graze, and accepted the offer. They picked up their bicycles—Nicholas managing to crack himself on the shin—and propped them by the fence. Nicholas' fell down again while he walked up the path, but he ignored it. He had had enough of his bicycle for some time.

"By the way," said the girl, as she thrust open the cottage door, "I'm Mildred Hyatt."

From the way she spoke Nicholas received an impression that she expected, or rather hoped, that he would recognize the name. But in the circles in which he moved this was a common trait, usually leading only to mutual embarrassment, so he merely replied, in much the same tone, that he was Nicholas Pounce. Miss Hyatt, however, was at once arrested.

"Then you're at the Old Manor? With Professor Pounce?"

"My uncle," said Nicholas, getting it over.

"But how thrilling!" cried Miss Hyatt. "I've read all his books. I think he's wonderful. Is he working down here?"

"No," said Nicholas. If he had had enough of the bicycle, he had had more than enough of the questionnaires. He looked anxiously at his hand, and Miss Hyatt, taking the hint, at once brought out iodine and liberally applied it. The result was extremely painful.

"I've some New-Skin as well," she said kindly. "Would you like that on top?"

Nicholas shook his head. He wanted to hop about to ease the pain, but this would have been too undignified, so instead he walked briskly round the room looking at the pictures on the walls. They were called "A Pair of Pets," "June," "Sweet Sixteen," and "Two Strings to Her Bow," all four titles being puns. The room itself was the average cottage parlour, except that it contained a portable gramophone and an upright piano, on which lay several sheets of music-paper and a work on Harmony.

"You compose?" said Nicholas, his manners returning as the pain diminished. "I thought I knew your name."

Mildred Hyatt flushed.

"Oh, that was nothing," she said. "Pure pot-boiling, in fact, and I'm rather ashamed of it. I'm working on something very different now."

"Are you?" said Nicholas, wondering what on earth it was that had brought Miss Hyatt fame. As has been said, he was very musical, and used to review gramophone records for the *Granta*, but in honest truth the name of Hyatt meant nothing to him at all. . . .

"A Modern Symphony," said Miss Hyatt. She corrected herself. "*Symphonie Moderne*. That's why I've come down here, to work on it. Of course I could just go on pot-boiling, and probably make a lot of money, but that's artistic suicide, don't you think?"

"Absolutely," agreed Nicholas. He began to feel really curious. The idea of any one of his own age making a lot of money always interested him, and moreover if Miss Hyatt composed popular songs, or popular dance tunes, he himself had a very pretty turn for sophisticated lyrics. So he hedged a bit by adding that some modern stuff, however wide in appeal, had really great merit. Gershwin, for instance. The words were usually too imbecile for—well, for words, but there was no reason why they should not be as witty as the melody. . . .

"Do you write yourself?" asked Miss Hyatt innocently.

Nicholas admitted that he did. If ever Miss Hyatt wanted a lousy little verse or two, just something to shove in quite tentatively, he wished she would let him know.

Mildred Hyatt looked at once eager and diffident.

"As a matter of fact," she said, "I *have* got a tune. Just one of my pot-boilers, you know, but rather effective."

"I wish you'd play it me," said Nicholas.

With a commendable lack of coyness she at once sat down to the piano. Nicholas was surprised. The tune was extraordinarily simple, without being in the least subtle. It tinkled. It went pom-tiddly-pom. In short, it was one of the dam' silliest tunes he had ever heard.

"Play it again," he said desperately, when she came to the end.

Miss Hyatt played it again, this time talking above the notes.

"It's nothing, of course," she said. (But Nicholas had a dreadful suspicion that her real opinion was quite different.) "Still, it would fit in with the second Suite, and I want to finish it. The first's still selling quite absurdly."

"By the way," said Nicholas, feeling that he had better know the worst, "have you got it here? The first Suite? I've never actually seen it."

Relinquishing the treble, Miss Hyatt reached down to a portfolio propped against the piano-side and extracted a slim, brightly covered album. Nicholas took it. The design outside represented a group of small children drawn in the manner of Mabel Lucie Attwell. They carried two banners, on one of which was inscribed "*Babies' Suite* (For Beginners)," and on the other "Mildred Hyatt." Below, more discreetly, appeared the words "First Prize B.B.C. Children's Hour Competition."

Miss Hyatt was now singing the melody to *la*. She was giving him plenty of time. Nicholas turned the pages, and saw that the suite consisted of four items, "Singing Sue," "Pussy Wash Dishes," "Tidy Tom," and "Willie Wolf-Cub." He glanced at the last:

> Willie, Willie Wolf-Cub,
> Come and lend a paw!
> You're the only sort of Wolf
> We DON'T keep from the door!

"Of course, the fuss was quite absurd," said Miss Hyatt, breaking off her *la's*, "and I photograph so badly, I simply loathed it. But I suppose if one *will* go in for public competitions one must take the consequences."

"Rather," agreed Nicholas, hoping he was not looking as sick as he felt.

"*Those* verses were written by a friend of mine, but she was frightfully shy about it all and wouldn't have her name mentioned. She's frightfully clever. Do you know, she did them all in about half an hour!"

"Did she, by Gum!" said Nicholas.

"I offered her half the prize, of course, but she wouldn't take it. She said she'd given me the verses and I was to put my own name to them. Of course I didn't do *that*, but I couldn't help getting the credit, and it rather worried me."

"Don't let it," advised Nicholas. "I know exactly how your friend felt."

Miss Hyatt looked grateful.

"But, of course, if *you* do any lyrics for me," she said, "it must be on a business footing. And you will, won't you? Because I really have rather a good idea, only I can't work it out. Listen!" She rapidly played the new melody through yet again. "What does that suggest?"

Since he did not like to say "A sick headache," Nicholas merely looked enquiring.

"Bluebells!" said Miss Hyatt positively. "'The Bluebell Princess.' And I thought I'd do a set of four—King, and Queen, and the Princess, and perhaps the Maids of Honour, and call it *The Bluebell Court*. Can't you just *see* the cover?"

Nicholas could. And he had to admit to himself that commercially the notion was a sound one.

"And you'll do the verses?"

Nicholas hesitated. He wanted some money badly, but at the same time he naturally flinched from associating himself—Nicky Pounce, the sophisticate of John's—with a *Babies' Suite*. It was out of character.

"Just *try*," said Miss Hyatt persuasively—and evidently reading his hesitation amiss. "I'm sure you could. And you needn't start with the Princess, if you get ideas for the others first. I mean, *I* might get suggestions from *you*."

"All right," said Nicholas, suddenly making up his mind. (After all, he could quite easily alter his character to include the toughly commercial: it would be rather funny.) "I'll do my best. But you mustn't expect anything as good as Willie Wolf-Cub."

"Yours will be better," affirmed Mildred Hyatt. "I'm simply dying to see them." She paused. Her manner changed. "Because I want to clear all this nonsense out of the way," explained Miss Hyatt rather consciously, "and get back to my *Symphonie Moderne*."

3

As he pushed his bicycle home again—he could not ride, because the handlebars were twisted—Nicholas found himself with a good deal to think about. He had become involved, if only intellectually, with a strange young woman: he had made a radical alteration in his own character, and thrust upon his Uncle Isaac the mantle of a trombonist: he had also had a bicycle accident and made friends with a Staffordshire Bull. It had been a full morning—and a double morning, passed half in the familiar air of Bloomsbury, half in the stranger atmosphere of the village; Nicholas drew a mental boundary at the end of Miss Hyatt's lane, and as he pushed his bicycle across it it struck him that the Gillenham climate had already undergone a change. No one now said "Mornin'" to him—possibly because they had said it already, but possibly because they had read the Professor's questionnaire. He saw one of the blue envelopes lying by the gutter—as though cast down in righteous wrath—and the sight depressed him. He hurried his pace, constantly hitting himself on the ankle with the near pedal; and behind him the cocks crowed with mirth.

At the Old Manor gate his uncle waited.

"Well?" said Professor Pounce briskly. "Have you delivered them?"

"Yes," said Nicholas. "Uncle Isaac, can you play the trombone?"

"No," said the Professor.

"Then I think you ought to learn. I dare say I could manage a few card-tricks . . ."

Professor Pounce did not reply. He wasn't listening; he was already gazing eagerly towards the village, as though expecting to see a stream of hurrying figures bearing completed questionnaires. He was not aware that in Gillenham no one ever read anything till nightfall, when darkness brought leisure for intellectual effort. The great majority of his blue envelopes lay still unopened beneath tea-caddies, coronation mugs, and other mantelpiece ornaments. Like time-bombs.

The day passed, and no completed questionnaires came in. Nicholas began to hope they never would. Before going to bed he went and stood as his uncle had done, looking up the lane; it was a beautiful night, smelling of earth and hay, and so still that not even the stars twinkled, but shone steadily as planets. Then a cock crew, and Nicholas started. Like most town-dwellers, he expected cocks to give voice only, and punctually, at dawn; he did not realize that they crowed whenever they felt like it, and the sound now struck him as strange and ominous. It was like a signal.

It was like a signal for something to begin.

CHAPTER 4

1

OVER the exterior of the village brooded a deep peace. What rare lights showed glimmered faintly between drawn curtains. The main street was as empty as the lanes, and almost as dark. From stable and byre came an occasional soft stirring of hooves in straw; from the upper rooms of the cottages a like, an almost responsive stir of sleep-heavy bodies in featherbeds.

The downstairs lights were at the Vicarage, where Mr. Crowner was making up the accounts of the Parish Magazine, at The Grapes, where Mrs. Jim Powley was rinsing glasses, and at Vander's Farm, where a mare had just foaled.

2

"Charles," said Mrs. Crowner, extracting the last sock from her mending-basket, "have you read that thing yet?"

"And two pounds nine and eightpence," murmured the Vicar. "What thing, my dear?"

"That questionnaire-thing from the Professor-person at the Old Manor. I gave it you at tea-time."

"No, I haven't," replied the Vicar. "Two pounds nine and eightpence. It's here in my pocket, and as soon as I have time—"

"Read it now, dear," directed his wife. "Read it at once—"

The Vicar wrote "One pound eight and ninepence" on a slip of paper, obediently took out the two sheets of Nicholas' typing and perused them with a growing interest.

"How very remarkable!" he ejaculated at last. "To think that we have lived here all these years—"

"I know it's remarkable," interrupted Mrs. Crowner quickly. "It—it's extraordinary. But that isn't the point. These questionnaire-things have been circulated all through the village, by the Professor's nephew. I saw him with my own eyes, on a bicycle, just as he left Mrs. Uffley's, and Mrs. Uffley at once gave me the thing to read, and of course as soon as I'd done so I said, 'It's just a circular, Mrs. Uffley,'—which in a sense it was, Charles, so you needn't look at me—and carried it away. But I don't know how many other people have had them, because I didn't like to make enquiries for fear of arousing undue interest."

"Well?" said the Vicar.

"The village may be—may be *sown* with the things!"

"If the young man took a bicycle," agreed Mr. Crowner, "it does seem probable that he visited more than one door."

"That's what I'm saying. The point is, Charles, what are you going to do?"

The Vicar reflected.

"I gather that no questionnaire was delivered here, and in any case I could not answer it beyond a first 'No.' You've never heard of the Stone of Chastity, have you?"

"Certainly not!" snapped Mrs. Crowner.

"I only thought that perhaps at the Women's Institute—"

"Certainly not!" cried Mrs. Crowner again.

"Then I don't see," finished the Vicar regretfully, "that we can do anything at all."

Mrs. Crowner put down her darning and clasped her hands tightly in her lap. She loved her husband with a fond and wifely love, but there were times when she found him exasperating.

"Charles, dear, please give your mind to this. That document is pagan. There is no other word for it. It is a deliberate attempt to arouse pagan memories."

"Professor Pounce," said Mr. Crowner gently, "would probably call it a piece of scientific research."

"I don't care what he calls it. Raking up the wicked past—"

"Like a Roman villa," murmured her husband.

"Romans were respectable," retorted Mrs. Crowner—rather arbitrarily. "This is not. If it doesn't arouse pagan memories, it will arouse pagan thoughts. It is your duty, Charles, to stamp it out."

"How, my dear?"

"With the Boy Scouts. They could go round first thing in the morning and collect them all up, and we could have a small bonfire in the kitchen-garden. I'm sure," added Mrs. Crowner, relaxing a little of her severity, "they'd enjoy it very much indeed."

"I'm sure they would," agreed the Vicar. "I'm sure they'd also enjoy reading the questions first. For the moment, my dear, I must ask you to leave the matter strictly alone."

Mrs. Crowner opened her mouth, and closed it again without speaking. She knew when she was defeated. To her alarmed and simple mind it seemed that the poison was already beginning to work.

"In any case," added the Vicar, casting one more look at the questionnaire, "if it makes any one of our flock seriously contemplate the subject of chastity, that will be more than all my sermons have ever achieved. One pound, eight shillings and ninepence."

3

"Jim!" called Mrs. Jim suddenly. "Ever heard tell of a Stone o' Chastity?"

"Stone o' what?" shouted Jim Powley.

"Chastity!" bawled Mrs. Jim, raising her voice. Her husband was in the cellar, but since this was his usual location while she tidied the bar, and since this was their best hour for domestic chat, they had formed the habit of shouting back and forth through the trapdoor. The Grapes stood detached from its neighbours, and the pot-boy slept out.

"No, I ain't," yelled Jim. "What is she?"

Mrs. Jim brought her apron up on to the freshly washed bar, folded her large arms comfortably upon it, and with complete unscrupulousness turned to Part II of the Professor's questionnaire before completing Part I.

"It's a stepping-stone, Jim, alleged to have the power o' testing female chastity. What d'you know about that?"

"Where is it?"

"Here in our brook. Leastways, seems it used to be in our brook, but now they're no so sure, an' that's what all these questions are about, because he wants to find out."

"Who does?"

Mrs. Jim's fat finger travelled slowly over the page. "Professor Pounce. Him that's took Old Manor." There was a short silence, then a clumping of feet, then Jim's head slowly rose through the open trap. It was the first time he had ever allowed the claims of conversation to interfere with a job.

"Well!" he exclaimed slowly. "That's a rum 'un! Who'd ha' thought it! The old randy!"

"It's got his name here plain as anything."

"You're sure 'tisn't the young 'un?"

"It says 'Professor.' If the one's too old, t'other's too young. What d'you make of it, Jim?"

Jim mounted a rung or two more, and heaved himself out, and came and leant on the other side of the bar. His wife twisted the pages sideways; and together, their lips moving in unison, they read laboriously through from beginning to end. Jim scratched his head. The academic detachment of the Professor's style had a damping effect.

"'Tis some nonsense o' the gentry's," he said at last. "That's all 'tis. I remember now, my Grannie used to get shillings from old Doctor for singing him bits of ancient songs. Here's the same sort o' thing, only this time 'tis fairy-tales."

"Well, what'll I do with it?"

"Do nothing," said Jim.

His wife folded the papers across and put them into an empty cocoa-tin where she kept loose slips for writing down grocery orders, beauty hints, and recipes for preserves. The bar was clean as a pin, but she did not as usual remove her apron and bang her way upstairs without waiting for Jim. Nor did her husband return to the cellar.

"I wonder if there *was*?" said Mrs. Jim softly.

"Not likely. Not in our time. What are you thinkin'?"

"I was thinkin'—if there *had* bin—the day I wedded you, bor, I'd ha' stepped across it proud as Punch."

The two heads, faded frizzy blond, rusty brown, bent close together.

"You would so," said Jim.

"There was some lasses round here—"

"There were so. *I* know that."

"And who better?" asked Mrs. Jim, not without a certain complacency. "But you never got round me, bor, till the ring was on my finger. Did you, bor?"

"I did not," said Jim. "You caught me fair and square."

An emotion as simple, as commonplace, as unpoetic as themselves brought their thick hands together over the scrubbed bar. Coarse and clean, like a scrubbed bar.

"Come to bed, old woman," said Jim lovingly. "I'll finish below in the morning."

He did not remember to shut the cellar trap, and early next day, Tom, the pot-boy, before he opened the shutters, fell down it. He was not badly hurt; but Mrs. Crowner would undoubtedly have seen in his fall a further justification of her attitude towards Professor Pounce.

4

"It's a colt," said Mr. Pye. "Likely, too. I'll take a small whisky."

At Vander's Farm they were teetotal and Nonconformist, within reasonable limits. That is to say, Mr. Pye drank whisky medicinally, and during a prolonged drought sent his wife to pray with the Anglicans. He needed physicking, however, considerably more often than his land needed rain.

"And Nelly?" asked Mrs. Pye.

"Nicely." The farmer supped his whisky, reflecting that each sup was costing him about threepence, and savouring it no less on that account. Mrs. Pye watched, and waited. A great soft moth blundered in towards the lamp; she shifted her gaze. The creature beat its plumy wings against the hot glass and dropped to the table; Mrs. Pye's hand shot out to crush it. Then she turned back to her husband and, when there were about four sups of the whisky left, silently placed in his free hand two typewritten sheets. (It is noticeable that it was commonly the women who brought Professor Pounce's questionnaire to the attention of their men.)

"Now, then!" protested Mr. Pye. "This is no time for catalogues!"

"'Tis no catalogue!" said his wife grimly. "Just you look at it before I put it on the fire."

Moved by much the same sentiments as those the Vicar feared in his Boy Scouts, Mr. Pye read.

"'Tis a scandal!" proclaimed Mrs. Pye. (It was a pity she did not always make one of the Vicar's flock: she and Mrs. Crowner would have found much in common.)

"I don't make head nor tail of it," said her husband. Like Jim at The Grapes, he found the Professor's style disappointing. "If you want to burn it, burn it, but what's amiss with chastity?"

"'Tis a double-edged sword," said Mrs. Pye. "Start thinking about chastity, and like as not you think about the other thing as well. That Blodgett creature—*Miss* Blodgett, indeed—she must ha' bin a brazen piece!"

Mr. Pye rather interestedly turned to the second page.

"I've not heard the name round these parts," he said. "But green garters, now—my Grannie had a pair. Knitted silk they were—"

"Then don't you say a word about them!" cried Mrs. Pye. She snatched the papers from his hand, crumpled them into a ball, and with a queer return of housewifeliness used it to wipe the crushed body of the moth from her shining table. Then she tossed it on the fire. "Don't you say a word!" she repeated. "I come from a respectable family, Thomas Pye—"

"There's nothing disrespectable about garters," retorted her husband. "Leastways, there wasn't in her day. My Grannie was a good woman."

He rose stiffly from his seat, loosened his shoulders, and went up to bed. But old, deep-buried memories were stirring in his mind; even after his wife had climbed in beside him and put out the light, and in spite of his fatigue, he did not sleep. He found he remembered his grandmother quite clearly: "good," he had called her, but when he came to think things over he discovered that he ought rather to have called her "kind." He could not recollect that she had ever shown any of the qualities he now considered proofs of virtue: she had not been particularly economical, nor strict after the maids, and she never made him go to church more than once a-Sunday, though her authority over him, after the death of his own mother, was in that line supreme. But she used to play children's games with him, and slip him apples, and knit mittens for his winter-bitten hands. And then when he came to man's estate, which was at the age of about twelve, she seemed suddenly to shrivel up into a little inconspicuous figure by the chimney-corner, so that he never afterwards paid much attention to her. He was too busy getting on in the world. "All work and no play," she once said, "makes Jack a dull boy"—which he considered very foolish indeed. . . .

"Pye, go to sleep," said Mrs. Pye sharply.

Mr. Pye turned on his side, counted three hundred sheep—black-faced Southdowns—and did as he was told.

There wasn't much wrong, in Mrs. Crowner's view, at Vander's Farm. At any rate, not yet.

5

The church clock struck twelve. In the houses already darkened the featherbeds stirred. A breath of wakefulness passed through the village. Wives and husbands, feeling the familiar conjugal warmth, opened one eye and slept again. The maidens stayed awake longer. One of the youths, twenty-year-old Arthur Cockbrow of Old Farm, put his feet out of bed, listened intently, and then crept softly up an attic stair to the room of his mother's maid.

"Sally! Let me in!"

There was a soft movement on the other side of the door. The breath had wakened Sally also.

"Sally! Let me in!"

The door opened, a mere crack. Mr. Cockbrow tried to put his foot in, but his toes were jammed.

"I daresn't, Master Arthur! Truly I daresn't!"

"You always say that," whispered Mr. Cockcrow crossly. "It's perfectly all right. Every one's asleep."

"It's not that, Master Arthur. Truly 'tisn't . . ."

"Sally, darling! Sally, you know how I love you. Don't you believe me?"

"Oh, I do, Master Arthur!" breathed Sally fervently. "It's not that . . ."

"Then what the hell is it?"

"The Government," whispered Sally. "There's papers all round the village, they're going to come down and try all us girls to find out—to find out *everything* . . ."

As well he might, Mr. Cockbrow took a few moments to reply.

"I don't believe it," he said. "It's utter nonsense. You've got hold of the wrong end of some stick."

"I haven't, Master Arthur. It's all there in printing. They're going to try all us girls, and—and oh, Master Arthur, I couldn't face it!"

Mr. Cockbrow pushed gently at the door.

"Let me in, Sally, and show me the paper, and I'll explain all about it."

But Sally was only nine tenths a fool. She pushed as gently but more firmly back. The lock of the door clicked.

"Sally!"

"I'll shout, Master Arthur! I will truly!"

"Sally, darling!"

"I'll shout for missus!"

"Damn," said Mr. Cockbrow.

No cajoleries prevailed. Considerably annoyed, even more puzzled, he stood there outside the shut door while his bare feet became unpleasantly conscious of the bare boards. He could not understand it at all. His pursuit of Sally had lasted a full two weeks—quite long enough to satisfy her pride—and had never looked in the least hopeless. And now in some mysterious way the Government had stepped in! The Government! It was lunatic!

"Sally!" called Mr. Cockbrow for the last time.

There was no answer. He felt instinctively that if he called till morning there would still be no answer. The Government had stepped in.

"Damn!" said Mr. Cockbrow; and went cautiously back to bed.

This episode would have puzzled Mrs. Crowner very much indeed.

CHAPTER 5

1

THE garden behind the Old Manor was an extremely pleasant place, and none the less so for being ill-kept. There were beds of poppies and lupins near the house, and bean-rows and peasticks and raspberry-canes beyond, and the poppies had seeded among the beans, and an occasional white peaseblossom showed among the lupins, and the grass of the lawn was no shorter or less tufted than the grass of the orchard behind the beanrows. When the wind blew, small hard apples dropped among the raspberries and made fresh holes in the unmended nets, and sometimes a peastick collapsed gently into the potato-bed, with a further mingling of blossoms, and the whole garden swayed in a state of gentle anarchy. The summer-house, which was also the tool-shed, either supported or was supported by a mass of clematis and blackberry-trails; under its circular wooden seat toadstools sprouted in interesting variety. Upon the seat, after a restless night, sat Nicholas Pounce.

He had a pencil in his hand, a writing-pad on his knee. For over an hour he had been wrestling with Miss Hyatt's lyrics, and they were much harder to do than he had anticipated. He had quite a turn for doubtful puns and polysyllabic rhymes, but an arch simplicity was beyond him. He tried again.

> The ladies of the Bluebell Court,
> Although no better than they ought
> To be, explain the Knave of Heart's
> Unbridled appetite for Tarts.

That was no good either. Nicholas tore the sheet from the pad and crumpled it into a ball. The trouble was that he couldn't concentrate. He was distracted. Though he had wisely determined to put the whole matter of the questionnaire from his mind, at any rate till its recipients made a move, he could not do so. Its recipients might make a move at any moment. He was also and more seriously distracted by thoughts of Carmen, to whom he desired to make love. Emotion being the life-blood of the artist, Nicholas felt that making love to Carmen was probably just what he wanted. He propped his feet against a rusty lawn-mower and tried again.

> The Bluebell King expects an heir—
> Let even Majesty beware!
> The Bluebell Queen, so rumours tally,
> Produced a Lily-of-the-Valley.

"Whatever are you at?" asked Carmen.

2

He looked up. She was there, in the arched doorway, with the blackberry sprays brushing her hair. His heart turned over once and then raced on.

"What *are* you at?" repeated Carmen.

"Nothing," said Nicholas. "Rubbish. Come in and talk to me."

Carmen considered him.

"What about?"

"Love," said Nicholas.

"All right," said Carmen. "Fire away."

Nicholas hesitated. There was a look in her eye he did not like. A sceptical look. . . .

"Love," declaimed Nicholas, "may be divided into two classes: sacred and profane. We will concentrate on the latter, and begin at the beginning: How would you describe, Miss Smith, the process of falling in love?"

Rather to his surprise, Carmen appeared to reflect a moment before answering.

"It's like going into a park," she said at last. "Before you go in you're just looking through the railings: you can still keep out if you want. That's when you've just met someone, or they've kissed you, and it's up to you to make the next move, and sometimes you don't know whether you want to or not. Because you can't see all the park, only the first lovely bits, and perhaps farther on there may be man-traps or bad animals, and perhaps you won't be able to get out again. So you don't know. And then you hear a fountain, or see the top of a summer-house, and you go in. And the gate shuts behind you. And there you are, a bit scared, but with all the exciting park to explore . . ."

Nicholas stared at her.

"Who told you?" he asked rudely.

"A man in a pub," said Carmen. "He was a bit blotto. Isn't it right?"

"Yes, it's right," said Nicholas. He looked at Carmen again, and saw wide bosomy lawns, rounded bosquets of trees, and the shrubberies that might conceal man-traps. "Did this fellow in the pub go in?" he asked.

"He *was* in," said Carmen. "He was in the bar."

"I meant into the park."

"It wasn't a real park, silly." Carmen looked so amused that Nicholas could only conclude that the language of metaphor was completely foreign to her. She had been repeating like a parrot.

"You've a wonderful memory," he said.

"Haven't I? I often bring that bit out when fellows start talking about love. It's ever so useful."

"And do any of the other fellows ask where you got it from?"

Carmen considered.

"Some do, and some don't. The ones that do mostly want to go on talking. I get sick of talk myself."

She stood up and stretched. Her extraordinary figure for an instant filled the doorway and blotted out the sky. Nicholas found himself on his feet, shaking a little with excitement. He put his hands one on either side of her waist: it was like grasping the slim trunk of a tree with the sap running; and like a tall tree she swayed towards him.

"You do kiss nicely," said Carmen.

Nicholas kissed her again.

"Like a real gentleman . . ."

Nicholas violently released her, and flung out of the summer-house, and went running, panting, swearing, through the garden, through the orchard, and out into the fields.

3

"Isaac, dear," said Mrs. Pounce, "I want to speak to you."

The Professor had a disconcerting trick of looking at her every now and again as though he were surprised to see her. He so looked at her now; it was only for a moment, but that moment sufficed to shake Mrs. Pounce's nerve.

"Isaac, *dear*!"

"Of course, of course," said the Professor, obviously addressing himself. "What is it, Maud?"

"I want to speak to you," said Mrs. Pounce. "Won't you sit down?"

"I've been sitting all morning," objected her brother-in-law, "waiting for those questionnaires to come in. I'll just take a stroll round."

"I can't speak to you while you're strolling, dear. I can't really."

The Professor plumped down in a chair, feet apart, hands on knees, and fixed her with his eye.

"Is that better?"

"No, it isn't!" cried Mrs. Pounce, now quite distracted. "All I ask is a little sympathetic understanding—"

"Damn!" said the Professor.

"Isaac!"

"I wasn't damning you," explained the Professor hastily. "I was damning those damned yokels. Some answers should surely have come in by now!"

Mrs. Pounce looked at him.

"Can't you think of *anything* else, Isaac?"

"No, I can't," replied the Professor frankly. "Where's that boy? Where's Nicholas? I believe I'll send him round to collect 'em."

"Listen, dear," said Mrs. Pounce. "I don't take up much of your time, in fact I'm a very self-effacing woman, but I really do need your attention just for once. Your dear brother—"

The Professor uttered a cry of exasperation.

"My dear Maud, I know all about my brother. He was one of the best men who ever lived. Good citizen, good husband, good father, and all the rest of it. A paragon of virtue. I have the greatest respect for his memory. In fact, his memory is so sacred to me that I must refuse to discuss him. Where's Nicholas?"

"I'll go and find him," said Mrs. Pounce sadly.

4

Lying on his face under a hedge Nicholas Pounce, who liked his women mature, could not make out what was the matter with him. The kissing of Carmen had disturbed him badly, and it had—felt Nicholas—no business to. He had simply bussed a wench in an arbour. But even the language of the eighteenth-century rake could not disguise the fact that as a rake he was something of a washout, and Nicholas wriggled in the grass with annoyance. Where on earth had Carmen acquired her standards of osculation? Not, surely, from the Professor? The notion was fascinating, but too improbable for serious consideration. The answer lay in the unknown, the unguessable hinterland of Carmen's private life.

"Park be blowed!" thought Nicholas. "It must be more like a jungle!"

To explore the jungle. . . .

He turned over on his back and stared up at a tangle of blackberry-stems. The unripe fruit was a dull red, rather the colour of Carmen's mouth. In spite of everything he decided that he very much wanted to kiss Carmen again. He decided that he would kiss Carmen again. He also decided that he must acquire more experience. It was too humiliating, at twenty-two, not to know everything about women. His thoughts turned to Mildred Hyatt. She was really quite attractive, a pretty little thing in her art-and-crafty style, and her situation at Rose Cottage would afford convenient privacy. . . .

Nicholas got up. The idea of making love to two young women at once restored his self-conceit; he could not now imagine what had sent him tearing through the garden like a mortified child. He felt extremely adult. Brushing the dust from his trousers, he deliberately returned. As he passed the summerhouse he noticed the ground still littered with balls of paper, and remembered the claims of the Bluebell Court. It would be well, in view of his designs on Miss Hyatt, to have some reasonable excuse for his next visit. (After the ice was broken, of course, there would be no need of excuses: Miss Hyatt would simply be waiting for him to come.) Nicholas re-entered the summer-house, and found his pencil and paper, and set to work.

There seemed no doubt that emotion was indeed the lifeblood of the artist. He was this time entirely successful:

Bluebells, bluebells, ring a fairy chime!
Her Majesty the Bluebell Queen
Wants to know the time.
One two, three four, four o'clock and one stroke more,
Ring across the fairy lea
And bring the Princess home to tea!

He did it in ten minutes flat, finishing just as his mother came seeking him through the garden.

5

"Collect 'em?" repeated Nicholas.

"Collect them," said the Professor firmly.

"Honestly, sir, it's too soon. You haven't given them a chance—"

"Collect any that are completed," said the Professor. "It's a fair walk out here from the village, and that may be a cause of delay."

"I'm sorry, sir, but I've damaged the bicycle."

"You have feet," said Professor Pounce.

CHAPTER 6

1

THE morning, however, was already far advanced; if Nicholas had had time to write four pieces of verse, and make love to Carmen, and suffer the consequences, Mrs. Crowner (for once disobedient to her husband) had had time to marshal her Boy Scouts and send them off scavenging for blue envelopes. Out of the original batch they retrieved forty-six: of the remaining four copies one was in Mrs. Jim's cocoa-tin, one was in ashes at Vander's Farm, one was under the girl Sally's pillow, and the fiftieth was in the bosom of Jim Powley's cousin, Mrs. Ada Thirkettle. This was accordingly the only specimen left for Nicholas to collect, and though Mrs. Thirkettle gave him a very odd look as she handed it over, he was so grateful to her that he bought three pots of her home-made damson jam. Mrs. Crowner acquired her batch for nothing: but then not one of her forty-six questionnaires had a word written on them.

2

"Only one!" cried the Professor indignantly.

"I'm afraid so, sir."

"But where are the rest?"

"The Boy Scouts got them."

"But why should the Boy Scouts want my questionnaire?"

"For Mrs. Crowner, sir. She's the Vicar's wife."

"But what on earth—" the Professor fairly leapt with impatience—"what on earth does Mrs. Crowner want with forty-nine copies?"

"I can't imagine, sir," said Nicholas untruthfully. "But as you've got one, hadn't you better look at that?"

Professor Pounce angrily pulled out the sheets and spread them on his desk. The next moment all anger, all impatience had vanished. He sat beatifically agape like a man before a celestial vision. Mrs. Thirkettle had filled in only one space, but that was enough. Opposite Question (a) —*"Have you ever heard of the Stone of Chastity?"*—she had written *"Yes"*.

Underneath, rather cramped but still legible, were three wonderful words more:

"In our scullery."

3

Nicholas rubbed his temple. He had bent down just as the Professor sat up, and their heads came into sharp contact. But Professor Pounce seemed not to have noticed. He sat transfixed, only his lips moving.

"God bless my soul!" murmured the Professor reverently.

"Well, I'm damned!" said Nicholas.

"In the scullery!" repeated the Professor. "In the humblest of domestic offices—"

"I suppose," said Nicholas, "it ought to be in a museum?"

"Not at all," said the Professor. "It ought to be in the brook."

The idea at first struck Nicholas as quite funny, as being one of the better of his uncle's mild jokes. But it was not. The Professor was perfectly serious; and as Nicholas realized this, amusement gave place to doubt.

"You mean you're going to try and shift it?"

"It's been shifted once," pointed out the Professor.

"Obviously, sir. But people don't like having their sculleries messed about."

'They like having their sculleries *improved*," said Professor Pounce. "The Stone is evidently part of a flagged floor: I have no doubt that the offer of a neat cement pavement, with the addition perhaps of a cork mat, would be very favourably received."

There was sometimes a certain practical wisdom about the Professor by which his nephew was always surprised. Nicholas tried another line.

"Won't that come rather expensive, sir?"

"I don't see why. A sack of cement can be obtained very reasonably, and you shall mix it and put it down. It will be an entertaining little piece of manual work which you will thoroughly enjoy."

"But look here, Uncle Isaac—"

"Which you will thoroughly enjoy," repeated the Professor firmly. "You had better come round with me now, and take the dimensions."

4

With the eager step of reckless enthusiasm the Professor marched down the village street. Several of the inhabitants were about, and the Professor hailed them all. "Good morning!" cried Professor Pounce. "Fine morning! Wonderful weather! How are the crops?"—to all of which greetings the inhabitants noncommittally replied "Ar." The Professor noted this with amusement, and when himself greeted by the Vicar, replied "Ar" in turn—or rather "Aha!" "And where are you off to?" asked the Vicar. "Aha!" replied Professor Pounce. . . .

To Nicholas, following sheepishly behind with his mother's tape-measure in his pocket, this frivolous behaviour was little short of revolting. Like all the very young he had a jealous eye for the perquisites, so to speak, of youth. Light-hearted abandon was one of them, and he suffered so deeply for his uncle's lack of dignity that he was almost glad to arrive at Mrs. Thirkettle's door.

5

"That's her," said Mrs. Thirkettle.

She, or it, was roughly two feet square, smooth, flat, in colour slightly darker than the rest of the paving-stones, and crossed by an irregular stain. A varying line of cement separated it from, and bound it to, its neighbours. It looked as though it had been in place a long time.

"So that's her," repeated the Professor reverently. "What is the mark?"

"Blood," said Mrs. Thirkettle.

"Dear me," said the Professor. "What—er—sort of blood?"

"Human," said Mrs. Thirkettle. "Our Pansy's. That was a cousin we had livin' here, a piece older than me she was, and she got done wrong by a soldier and cut her throat. And she meant to do it over the sink, but what with the natural excitement, and never having done such a thing before, she messed up the flags instead. And that stone being just underneath, scrub as we might we couldn't get it clean. Mother *was* upset."

"I can well imagine it," said the Professor.

"But Pansy being her own brother's youngest, she said it could be a sort of memorial like, and a warning to us girls not to go wrong."

"And a very forcible one," agreed the Professor. "But how do you know that this is what used to be known as the Stone of Chastity?"

"Why, because Dad fetched her out o' Bowen's brook when they put the new bridge across. He'd had his eye on her for years and years, along of the one here being so wore down. She just fitted nicely."

"I can see that. But what made you think it was the Stone?"

"Grandma said so. She lived with us too, and when Dad came home she had a real good laugh. 'Now you *have* done something, bor,' she said. 'That's the Stone o' Chastity, that is, bin in Bowen's since Domesday.' And she used to come and look at it, laughing her silly old head off."

"I expect she told you many a tale about it?" suggested the Professor hopefully.

"Not her. She told no tales, Grandma didn't, 'less old Doctor give her a shilling for 'em."

Professor Pounce hesitated. There was evidently a stronger commercial strain in the Thirkettles than he had anticipated.

"Well, I'll give you five shillings for that stone," he said. "Just as a curiosity. My nephew here will take it up—"

"An' ruin my scullery floor! He won't," said Mrs. Thirkettle.

"It shall be replaced by a neat patch of cement. And a cork mat. You will find it a great improvement," said the Professor persuasively.

Mrs. Thirkettle hesitated in turn.

"Five shillings still ain't enough. That stone's historical, that is. I dare say I could get pounds and pounds for her."

"Have you ever had an offer before?"

"Can't say as I have," admitted Mrs. Thirkettle.

"Then let me tell you, you never will again. I can pick up that sort of stone all over the country."

"But not with Pansy's blood on 'em," pointed out Mrs. Thirkettle. "That's a memorial, that stone is, and I often look at her."

The Professor felt in his pocket and produced a handful of silver.

"Seven-and-six," he bargained. "Seven-and-six, a cement patch and a cork mat. You can take it or leave it."

"Fifteen shilling."

Professor Pounce turned towards the door.

"Ten shilling!"

Professor Pounce turned back.

"Right," he said. "My nephew will be round in the morning. Just measure for the mat, Nicholas, and we will leave Mrs. Thirkettle in peace."

6

"Now that," said the Professor, as they retraced their steps, "is what I call a thoroughly satisfactory transaction."

"I don't," said Nicholas priggishly. "I feel rather sick. That poor kid Pansy—"

*"Most suggestive!" cried the Professor joyously. "She must have committed suicide actually on the Stone. The Stone, so to speak, found her out."

They had reached the narrow lane leading to the Old Manor gates. No one was in sight. Nicholas turned and faced his uncle.

"Look here, sir," he demanded, "do you actually believe in this thing?"

The Professor considered.

"I don't know," he said at last. "I really don't know. My mind is in a state of not unpleasurable confusion. But we shall soon see."

"How?"

"By experiment, of course," said the Professor impatiently. "You don't suppose that after this phenomenal stroke of luck I shall let the matter rest? The Stone shall be replaced in Bowens brook—perhaps with some little ceremony—the candidates shall approach in turn—"

Nicholas clutched his relative by the arm.

*"What candidates, Uncle Isaac? *Who* will approach?"

"Any one who cares to enter, of course. I shall invite all the village women to begin with, by means of a notice posted on the church door."

Nicholas was speechless.

"And if we get a good entry," continued Professor Pounce, springing in his walk as the notion expanded and took more and more elaborate shape, "we will make case-histories of each candidate and analyse the results. It will be one of the most remarkable pieces of research since Fraser. You don't seem to realize your luck."

Nicholas realized a good many things; but his own special good fortune was not one of them.

CHAPTER 7

1

THERE was no cement to be had in Gillenham.

To take up a bedded paving-stone was highly skilled work.

To refill the gap with cement (supposing such to be procurable, which it was not) and make a neat job of the whole was work more highly skilled still.

These conclusions were presented to Nicholas next morning by a committee of three—one Fox, one Uffley, and one Thirkettle—which Nicholas encountered, apparently in permanent session, outside the closed doors of The Grapes. While waiting for those doors to open the trio were quite ready to give Nicholas the benefit of their advice. Their several ages added up to about two hundred and sixteen, and their outlook was pessimistic.

"Then where *can* I get cement?" demanded Nicholas.

"Ipswich," replied Mr. Fox, "That's a dam great way, that is."

"Isn't there a bus or something?"

"Goes Tuesdays and Saturdays," said Mr. Uffley.

"Well, it's Saturday to-day," said Nicholas hopefully. "Where does it start from?"

"It's gone," said Mr. Fox.

They all contemplated this deadlock for some minutes. Then Mr. Thirkettle dreamily spoke.

"That's a dam great cinema they got at Ipswich. . . ."

"Ar," said Mr. Uffley.

Nicholas looked desperately up and down the street. He had already tried the single shop, which stocked bull's-eyes, boots, bootlaces, dry goods, tinned salmon and wire netting, but did not stock cement. The three elders looked into space. They all knew why Nicholas wanted cement—Mr. Thirkettle was actually Ada Thirkettle's brother-in-law—and were really taking an immense interest in the subject; but they looked like nothing so much as three old tortoises stretching their horny necks in the sun.

"I suppose there isn't anything I could use instead?" hazarded Nicholas.

"Not if you want to do the job proper," said Mr. Uffley severely.

"And a dam great organ," mused Mr. Thirkettle. "I'd ha' bin glad to take me boots off."

Nicholas turned desperately to Mr. Fox.

"You're certain there's nowhere nearer than Ipswich, sir?"

The appeal was well timed. Mr. Fox, despite his age, possessed an abnormally quick ear, which at that moment detected the first stirring of life inside The Grapes public bar. The amusement afforded by Nicholas was therefore no longer necessary to him.

"Try young Arthur," said Mr. Fox, cautiously flexing his ancient limbs in preparation for a move.

"Who's young Arthur?"

"Wheelwright," said Mr. Fox. "'Cross the way. We bin standing plumb opposite his dwelling all this while."

2

To Nicholas' relief young Arthur turned out to be no more than forty-five, and not only a wheelwright but a plumber, joiner, and bricklayer as well. He was a large man, rather noble-looking, like a Newfoundland. Cement, either to procure or to lay, presented no difficulty to him. He had a sack of it actually in his yard. But when the nature of the job was explained to him, he looked grave. Quite frankly, he doubted whether Nicholas could handle it. In fact, his doubts were so grave that he positively refused to sell Nicholas any of his cement.

"'Twould be plain robbery," declared young Arthur earnestly. "Dam mucky stuff as 'tis, there's an art in mixing can't be learnt nor taught save after years and years. . . ."

Nicholas hesitated. He had a pretty strong notion that he could learn to mix cement if not in an hour, at least in an afternoon: but how was he to set about it if he couldn't get the cement to mix?

"Chipping out that stone, now," continued the wheelwright. "That's a perilous task for you! Dam great splinters flying up, hit you in the eye, black patch or worse to the end of your days! I once see a bloke coffined with the patch still on him . . ."

"Did you?" said Nicholas.

"I did so. 'Twas a sight to make angels scoot. I'll lay when Peter saw him coming he said, 'Rightabout, bor! You're for the little old gentleman below!'"

All this seemed to Nicholas to be looking rather far ahead; but he had in truth no great anxiety to tackle the upheaval of the Stone. He had once hit his thumb very painfully with a hammer while merely opening a packing-case. Moreover, although young Arthur was regarding him with the eyes of a Newfoundland imploring its master not to attempt a dangerous peak, he began to suspect that this solicitude was not wholly disinterested.

"How much?" he asked bluntly.

At once young Arthur's fine benevolent brow cleared. He looked as though a great weight had been taken off his mind. He pondered.

"There's getting it up," he began, "and there's carting it, and there's carting the cement—"

"How much?" repeated Nicholas.

"Thirty bob," said young Arthur.

He looked so wounded, and so noble in his hurt, that Nicholas could not bring himself to haggle. He knew the price was outrageous, and that his uncle would never refund, but he had had enough.

"Right," he said. "When can you do it?"

"Monday," said young Arthur—still a little pained.

Nicholas nodded, and turned towards the door. On the threshold he paused. He had noticed a small card hanging from the door-knob. *"Arthur Fox,"* it said, *"Wheelwright and Joiner."*

"By the way," asked Nicholas, "old Mr. Fox, the man I was talking to outside The Grapes—the one who sent me to you—is he any relation?"

"He's my Dad," said young Arthur simply.

3

Nicholas emerged on to the sunny doorstep, and at once was confronted by a fresh problem. (His life at this time was full of interest, but rather tiring.)

Directly opposite him, outside The Grapes, stood Carmen Smith. She was bareheaded, and in the strong sunlight her hair shone like brass. She wore a rather full cotton skirt, dark blue, and a lighter blue jersey that stretched tightly across her breasts. She was a very noticeable figure.

Nicholas hesitated. Much as he desired Carmen's company in general, he could always do without it in the village. She aroused too much interest: she did more, she aroused too much emotion. The men stared at her with an odd, embarrassed sheepishness, the women with frank antagonism. The women had hated Carmen on sight.

"I'd better get her home," thought Nicholas, with vague uneasiness. Carmen was standing there quietly, passively, blocking no one's path, doing no harm to any one, and yet he had a feeling that she might at any moment start a riot. Two women passed by, and turned to stare; Carmen, gazing straight over their heads, appeared not to notice them. Nor did she notice the two hobbledehoys leaning against the wall. But as Nicholas moved off his doorstep he saw her head turn. A middle-aged man, big-boned, iron-grey, as tall as herself, was coming towards her; possibly through the accident of their eyes being on the same level, Carmen saw him. It was a positive, not a passive act. The man, who looked like a substantial farmer, stopped dead. Nicholas saw him say something, and saw Carmen answer. He himself was half across the road, and there seemed nothing for it but to go on and join them.

"Hello," said Carmen. "We're going to have a drink. This is Mr. Pye."

"I know your uncle," said Mr. Pye. "He's very interested in ferrets."

This was a new light on the Professor, and Nicholas looked surprised.

"Ferrets?" he repeated.

"Ferrets," said Mr. Pye.

There was a considerable pause. Neither Carmen nor her new friend moved. They were both quite obviously waiting for Nicholas to take himself off. But Nicholas wasn't going. He had remembered who Mr. Pye was—the biggest farmer of the district, much married to the President of the Women's Institute—and felt that the seed of his imaginary riot was being sown under his eye.

"In that case," he said idiotically, "the drinks ought to be on me. On the ferrets, in fact . . ."

Over his head—he wished they were not both so much taller than himself—a look passed.

"Thanks," said Mr. Pye, and led the way into the private bar.

4

There was no one else present save Mrs. Jim, who looked at the trio with great interest. Nicholas ordered the drinks—port and lemon, pint of bitter, half of mild—and Mr. Pye fetched his own and Carmen's to a small table before a settle on which there was room only for two persons, leaving Nicholas to hover at the bar.

"And how's your uncle?" asked Mrs. Jim affably.

"Oh, fine," said Nicholas.

"He must be a very interesting man," said Mrs. Jim. "From all we hear of him . . ."

"He's interesting all right," said Nicholas.

Mrs. Jim's reflective eye lighted on Carmen.

"Any relation?"

"Miss Smith helps the Professor with his work," said Nicholas.

"She's got a fine figure," said Mrs. Jim.

Nicholas took a larger throatful of beer than he intended, and choked. He did not think Carmen could hear: Mrs. Jim had lowered her voice to a professional barmaid whisper, directed at one individual ear; and in any case Carmen would probably not have minded. But Nicholas, super-sensitive, glanced anxiously round.

Carmen was not drinking, nor was Mr. Pye. They were not speaking. They were simply sitting, jammed close together, their thighs touching, on the narrow settle. Now and then they looked at each other, and Carmen smiled her slow, still smile. Mr. Pye did not even smile back: he merely stared. But their immobility was not reposeful: it was full of latent force. Carmen, standing alone on the pavement outside, had given the same impression; now it was doubled. The thing was fantastic, but every time Carmen smiled, every time

Mr. Pye stared, Nicholas felt the whole social structure of the village quiver as before an earthquake.

"Well, I mind my own business," said Mrs. Jim irrelevantly.

Nicholas walked over to the settle.

"Another drink, Carmen?"

Carmen shook her head.

"Mr. Pye?"

Mr. Pye shook his head also.

"I think," said Nicholas desperately, "we'd better be getting home to lunch."

"I'll follow," said Carmen.

But Mr. Pye lifted his tankard and poured its contents down his throat, and at once Carmen, as though in obedience to an unspoken order, drained her glass. (Nicholas wished he could handle her in the same way.) They stood up. The farmer nodded to Mrs. Jim, and with a hand on Carmen's hip propelled her towards the door.

"Your change!" called Mrs. Jim.

Nicholas, close on their heels, turned back to the bar. He was furious. He had paid for the drinks, and never been so ignored in his life, and the expression in Mrs. Jim's eye, of almost maternal sympathy, simply made things worse.

"Thanks," he said curtly.

But Mrs. Jim did not immediately hand over his silver.

"Mr. Pounce—" she began.

"You needn't tell me," said Nicholas bitterly. Then he looked at her fat philosophic face and suddenly saw in her a potential ally. "Look here," he said, "can't *you* speak to her?"

"I mind my own business," repeated Mrs. Jim. "But this I will say, bor. I like you, I like your uncle. The only time he was in here he was very polite to me. Your mother looks like a real lady. But Mrs. Pye's a Fury."

"Go on," said Nicholas.

"She keeps her old man on a tight rein. This is the first time I've ever known him break out. I can see why, bless you: there's some women, like *her*, that if a man takes a fancy to drive all else out of his mind. Mr. Pye's a strong man."

"Then he won't be driven," said Nicholas hopefully.

"He's strong on what he wants," said Mrs. Jim. "If Mrs. Pye can't master him she'll take it out somewhere."

"She can't *do* anything . . ."

"She can set fire to Old Manor and burn you all in your beds," said Mrs. Jim cheerfully. "Mind, I don't say she will, but I've no doubt she'd like to. And I don't know how much store your uncle sets by these fairy-tales of his, but she'll bitch up all that. She'll put stories about so that no one will dare have truck with him. She'll put stories about about you and that Miss Hyatt—"

"Oh, Lord!" groaned Nicholas.

"She will. She's got a tongue like an adder. You be warned, bor . . ."

"It's all very well warning me—" began Nicholas, and suddenly turned towards the door. Carmen and Mr. Pye had been at least three minutes unchaperoned. Leaving his change behind again, he almost ran after them.

5

But Carmen was alone, standing just as he had seen her half an hour earlier—head up, eyes unblinking, in the strong sunlight.

"You've kept me waiting," she stated. "First you hustle me out, then you keep me waiting."

Nicholas ignored this.

"Where's Mr. Pye?"

"Gone off in his car. If you hadn't kept me waiting we could have got a lift. I dare say if we hurry we could catch him by the Post Office."

"We're going to walk," said Nicholas.

They set off in uncompanionable silence, Nicholas urgently revolving in his mind methods of passing on the wisdom of Mrs. Jim. There seemed nothing for it but plain speech.

"Look here," he said, "if I were you, I shouldn't see so much of Mr. Pye."

Carmen looked extremely amused.

"I haven't seen him at all. Not before."

"You mean that was the first time—?"

"Well, I'd *seen* him," admitted Carmen. "But not to speak to. And he's seen me, but not to speak."

Nicholas was impressed in spite of himself.

"Well, I shouldn't have thought it," he said.

"I dare say not," agreed Carmen.

They walked on a bit farther.

"Anyway," said Nicholas, "I shouldn't see any more of him."

"Why not?"

There was no use, with Carmen, in beating about the bush.

"Because he's got a wife who won't like it. She's got a very violent temper."

"So have I," said Carmen thoughtfully.

"Then that's all the more reason why you should avoid rows."

"I don't mind rows," said Carmen.

"Well, other people do. And it won't be only your row, it will be Professor Pounce's row as well. If Mrs. Pye gets her back up she can probably mess all his work—everything he's come down here to do. You say he pays you to help; I've never noticed you helping much, but at least you needn't be a hindrance."

Rather to his surprise, this appeal had some effect. But he had observed before that Carmen always took money very seriously. It appealed, in a sense, to her best instincts.

"I'd be sorry to spoil his fun," she admitted.

"Well, you will if you're not dam careful."

"All right," said Carmen. "I'll take care."

Looked back on afterwards, this answer was not entirely reassuring; but at the moment Nicholas felt he had done rather well. The atmosphere became more friendly. By the time they reached the turning in Manor Lane Nicholas had not only forgiven Carmen her brazenness, but was once more desirous of kissing her; and Carmen made no objection.

6

Had Nicholas been more familiar with rural life he would have known where, before such a social earthquake as he glimpsed, to look for the first crack. There was a meeting of the Women's Institute that same afternoon.

These meetings were at no time dull. There were too many subterranean goings-on. There was the perennial battle for leadership between Mrs. Crowner and Mrs. Pye, there was the perennial and slanderous battle between Mrs. Uffley and Mrs. Ada Thirkettle, both of whom had daughters of a certain notoriety. Maternal pride is a great sharpener of the wit, and there was little to choose between them as mistresses of innuendo. There was also Mrs. Jim, whose freedom of tongue, no less than the number of her new hats, united even Thirkettle and Uffley in a common front.

Every one enjoyed the meetings very much.

At the moment Mrs. Crowner was on top, for she had induced all members to sew, knit or cut out for her Chinese

Mission (materials provided out of the collection on Rogation Sunday) and this lent to the gathering a definitely Church of England atmosphere which put Mrs. Pye and her sister Nonconformists slightly at a disadvantage. But Mrs. Pye was by no means out of action.

"I hear," she said smoothly, "Vicar's made quite a friend of Mr. Pounce?"

"Hardly a *friend,*" said Mrs. Crowner, smiling. "I believe he's spoken to him in the road. Who's ready for another chemise?"

"And Miss Smith," added Mrs. Pye, "Miss Carmen Smith, she calls herself . . ."

"I don't believe he's even spoken to *her*," said Mrs. Crowner.

"Just as well, maybe," mused Mrs. Fletcher. (She was Mrs. Pye's permanent toady, and earned her scraps.)

"The old 'uns are the jealousest of the lot," proceeded Mrs. Pye. "I know Vicar don't need my advice—"

"No?" smiled Mrs. Crowner.

"—but if he asked for it, I'd say, let her alone."

Mrs. Crowner's smile had become a fixed muscular contraction.

"I mean, of course," added Mrs. Pye, "in the way of religion."

The Vicar's wife was a Christian woman. There was nothing for her to do but take the chemise in her hand and walk away in search of Mrs. Jim. A teetotaller herself, it sometimes bothered her that she should so often be forced into alliance with the publican's wife.

"Put it down," said Mrs. Jim cheerfully. "I'll deal with it." She raised her voice so that it easily carried down the hall. "We had Mr. Pye in this morning," she said. "Looked pretty bobbish for once."

"Did he?" said Mrs. Crowner weakly.

Mrs. Jim nodded. The cornflowers in her hat nodded also. It was a hat from Ipswich.

"Better than I've seen him in years. Almost cheerful, he looked. As though he'd got a new interest in life."

At the other end of the hall Mrs. Pye whirled violently at her sewing-machine.

"I've always felt sorry for him, some ways," continued Mrs. Jim. "He never seemed to get much pleasure. Men want a bit o' pleasure now and then."

"And they mostly get it," put in Mrs. Thirkettle darkly. She had not meant to agree with Mrs. Jim, but she could not resist so obvious a truism. To re-establish her belligerent status she looked disapprovingly at the cornflowers, and added that some women didn't do so bad neither.

"The young 'uns will be young," observed Mrs. Jim blandly. "Now, your Sally—"

"Ah!" said Mrs. Uffley.

Mrs. Thirkettle rounded on her.

"My Sally's in good service!"

"At Old Farm," mused Mrs. Uffley.

"And where better? Two girls besides, and Mrs. Cockbrow a fine housekeeper!"

"And Master Arthur a fine young cockerel. . . . No, you go to Ipswich, I said to my Grace, and take service with the gentry. There's no one round here for *you*."

"And back she came a month later," added Mrs. Thirkettle. "If it's chopping and changing she likes, she's got it."

Mrs. Jim, the diversion created, placidly bit off the last thread of her current chemise and started in to tack the new one. Mrs. Crowner, still standing beside her, looked worried. Such personal exchanges were just the sort of thing she set her face against, and she wished, not for the first time, that the neighbourhood could furnish more didactic talent. If there were only some one at each meeting to talk about bees, or hand-looms, or Romans, or any other safe uncontroversial subject! But Mr. Bryce, from Ipswich, had given his lecture on Roman Remains three times already, and the Vicar had spoken twice on Old East Anglia, and the lady from the Village Industries Bureau always wanted her expenses. . . .

"I wish we could get somebody to *talk* to us!" murmured Mrs. Crowner absently.

It was Miss Hyatt who said it. Miss Hyatt, who had come in to ask the Vicar's wife whether she might use the Vicarage telephone, and who was now standing over Mrs. Crowner as Mrs. Crowner stood over Mrs. Jim. . . .

"Why don't you ask Professor Pounce?" suggested Miss Hyatt.

At once the whirr of the sewing-machine stopped, at once all needles, all knitting-pins were suspended.

"Why don't you ask the Professor?" repeated Miss Hyatt innocently. "He's terribly distinguished. He could tell you all about the old legends—"

She broke off, suddenly aware of a peculiar quality in the attention of her listeners. Their silence was more than polite, it was unnatural. You could have heard a pin drop. She looked enquiringly at the Vicar's wife, and Mrs. Crowner flushed.

"I don't think, my dear, we want to hear anything about *that*."

"About what?" asked Miss Hyatt.

Before Mrs. Crowner could answer—and indeed she had no answer ready—Mrs. Uffley coughed. It was a meaning, a pointed cough, the sort of cough to rivet attention.

"If it's the Stone o' Chastity," she observed, her eye again on Mrs. Thirkettle, "there's some here have heard about it already. There's some here ha' made ten shilling out o' it . . ."

7

Now, every one in the village knew about Mrs. Thirkettle's deal with Professor Pounce—every one, that is, except Mrs. Crowner. This made the situation very interesting: they were all anxious to see how the Vicar's wife would take it. Public opinion as a whole was behind Mrs. Thirkettle: the gentry were fair game, you made what you could out of them: but there were also advantages in being in with the Vicarage, and the Thirkettle support was not solid. The nucleus of the opposition, consisting of Mrs. Pye and her satellite, Mrs. Fletcher, was solid as a rock.

For a moment the Vicar's wife did not comprehend. She had not caught the whole phrase, and looked at Mrs. Uffley with bright enquiry.

"Ten shillings? Who's made ten shillings?"

"Ada Thirkettle," said Mrs. Uffley.

"But that's splendid! How did you make it, Ada? Honey?"

"She made it," said Mrs. Uffley, "selling o' the Stone o' Chastity to Mr. Pounce."

"Ada!" cried Mrs. Crowner; then as the full implications of the statement came home to her her jaw fell, and she gazed at Mrs. Thirkettle in speechless horror. All in vain had she sent out the legion of her Boy Scouts, all in vain had she personally superintended the bonfire in the kitchen-garden: the poison was out, it was working, already it had corrupted one of the hitherto more-or-less upright Thirkettles. So at that first moment ran Mrs. Crowner's thoughts; the good woman did not suspect more than a piece of mere commercial dishonesty. "Ada!" she repeated. "How *could* you!"

"'Twasn't doing no good where 'twas," defended Mrs. Thirkettle sulkily.

"Where it was? Where was it?"

"In our scullery," said Mrs. Thirkettle.

"Pansy's blood still fresh to be seen," added Mrs. Uffley, with relish. "I'd as soon sell my mother's coffin."

"For ten shilling, there's some 'ud sell their grannie's bones," put in Mrs. Jim sharply. Ada Thirkettle was her husband's cousin, and though they commonly sparred like cats on a wall, any major issue brought them into alliance. Her hit was shrewd, Mrs. Uffley being a notorious skinflint who had sold her late husband's clothes before he was under ground; but it did not help to enlighten the Vicar's wife.

"I don't know what you're talking about!" said Mrs. Crowner, quite angrily. "But if Ada Thirkettle sold Mr. Pounce a paving-stone out of her scullery for ten shillings, she ought to be ashamed of herself."

"He offered," said Mrs. Thirkettle sullenly.

"Then that just shows that poor Mr. Pounce isn't quite right in his head, and you oughtn't to have taken advantage of him." Despite the severity of her words, Mrs. Crowner looked suddenly more cheerful. The theory that Professor Pounce was insane (a theory which, during the course of his career, had occurred to several other of the Professor's acquaintances) enabled her to take a more charitable view of him. He didn't know what he was doing. Also, if he were actually certifiable, there must be someone with authority over him, someone who, if he really Broke Out, could be made to come and take him away. But scarcely was this happy notion formulated in Mrs. Crowner's brain, when Mildred Hyatt rudely destroyed it.

"Nonsense!" cried Miss Hyatt. "I'm sorry, Mrs. Crowner, but really that's absurd! Professor Pounce is one of the most distinguished scholars living. Not quite right in the head—it's simply too preposterous!"

"Isn't it equally preposterous," retorted Mrs. Crowner, "to pay ten shillings for a common flagstone?"

"For a common flagstone, maybe," cut in Mrs. Thirkettle. "For the Stone o' Chastity I call it dam cheap. The truth is, I bin done down."

Mrs. Crowner collected her wits. She had made, as she now realized, an initial mistake in attaching too much importance to Mrs. Thirkettle's commercial honesty. There were graver issues at stake.

"I want every one to understand," she said, "to be quite sure, that this talk of a Stone of—of Chastity is completely untrue. No such thing exists—"

Like a boomerang, her mistake came back.

"It does so!" affirmed Mrs. Thirkettle doggedly. "*I* didn't do down Professor, 'twas Professor downed me."

"We won't go into that again, Ada. No such object exists—"

"'Twas the Stone he asked for, and the Stone he got," continued Mrs. Thirkettle. "My Grannie said so. 'That's the Stone o' Chastity,' she said, 'bin in Bowen's Brook since Domesday.' And my Grannie was a truthful woman."

She looked round defiantly: Mrs. Jim—since Ada Thirkettle's grandmother was Jim's grandmother also—nodded vigorous agreement. Mildred Hyatt impulsively ranged herself at their side. Her eager imagination saw them as battling for the tradition of Old England against an unsympathetic modernism. (This was very hard on Mrs. Crowner, who had done as much as any woman in the country to promote communal folk-dancing.)

Up behind Mrs. Crowner stepped Mrs. Pye. She had not spoken for some time, but all were acutely conscious of her dark censorious presence. She spoke now.

"Abhorred of the Lord and stinking to man," said Mrs. Pye. "A wicked heathen image. That's what your Stone is, Ada Thirkettle: and your ten wicked shillings'll turn to ashes in your mouth and stones to break your teeth, and vipers to sting you in your evil bosom."

This energetic support did not please Mrs. Crowner as much as might have been expected. She felt Mrs. Pye's language to be exaggerated; moreover, instead of denying the existence of the Stone outright (in Mrs. Crowner's view by far the best course) Mrs. Pye had simply given it fresh importance. However, she was definitely anti-Chastity—here Mrs. Crowner had quickly to correct her thought—anti-Thirkettle, and as such had perforce to be accepted as an ally.

The opposing parties now stood clearly defined; and before the ruck of the commonalty lay a hard choice. The Pyes at Vander's, after the Cockbrows of Old Farm, were the largest employers of labour in the district; Mrs. Crowner's influence, particularly in the matters of reference-giving to maidservants and the browbeating of reluctant bachelors, was very great. But on the other side stood Mrs. Jim, wife of Jim Powley, landlord of The Grapes. Mrs. Jim's charity was almost as lavish as Mrs. Crowner's, and far less discriminate. The Grapes was the only place in Gillenham where one could get a bet put on a horse. The Grapes was, above all, Gillenham's only source of beer; and the landlord of a free house has practically absolute power to regulate supplies. If Jim Powley chose to say a man was drunk, and to refuse to serve him, were that man sober as a judge he wouldn't get a drop out of Jim. Through the mind of every wife who loved her husband all these considerations urgently passed. Mrs. Thirkettle and Miss Hyatt were simply ignored: Mrs. Jim alone it was who Atlas-like upheld the reputation of Grandma Powley and the legend of the Stone.

"Them that believes in such wickedness," observed Mrs. Fletcher loudly, "did ought to be wholly ashamed of themselves."

This was only to be expected, for Mrs. Fletcher was Mrs. Pye's permanent toady. Mrs. Tom Uffley, whose husband was the Pye cowman, nodded assent.

"Them that calls their neighbours cheats and liars," countered Mrs. Fox, "did ought to be wholly ashamed also." (Her husband worked for Vander's, but her son Tom was pot-boy at The Grapes.)

With horror, with bewilderment, poor Mrs. Crowner saw the happy and united assemblage splitting before her eyes into two camps. Broadly speaking, the Old Farm people backed Mrs. Jim and the Vander's people backed herself, though there were one or two renegades like the last speaker, Mrs. Fox, and widowed Mrs. Brain, whose daughters Mabel and Violet were employed by Mrs. Pye, while her brother was employed by the Cockbrows. (It was noticeable that religious and family tics had less weight than economic.) Mrs. Crowner could not think how it had all come about.

"We all," she said, not very hopefully, "seem to be making an absurd fuss over nothing." She glanced at the clock: time was her only true ally, the meeting was within a few minutes of its end. "If I've hurt Ada's feelings I'm sure I'm very sorry, and I hope she'll forgive me."

These conciliatory words aroused no enthusiasm. They fell upon the dead silence like lumps of cold pudding.

"It's all over," continued Mrs. Crowner desperately, "and we needn't think any more about it. Need we?"

(In his study at the Old Manor Professor Pounce was even then making plans for his public Trial of Chastity.)

"And I think it would be very nice," finished Mrs. Crowner, "as time's nearly up, if we ended this meeting straight away with some community singing. 'John's Brown's Body'!"

Without waiting for an answer she produced her tuning-fork, quickly struck it, and immediately led off. Oddly enough, the response was terrific. It sounded almost like part-singing. Urgently beating time, Mrs. Crowner received the impression that one half of her choir was trying to race the other. And they wouldn't stop. They repeated the song over and over again, louder and louder, till it sounded like the battle-cry it was. Only they weren't all singing the same words.

Mrs. Crowner never knew who started it, but one half of her choir, the half that was winning, had found a revised version,

> "Grandma's body lies a-mouldering in the grave,
> Grandma's body lies a-mouldering in the grave,
> GRANDMA'S body lies a-mouldering in the grave,
> But her soul goes marching on!"

"That will do!" said Mrs. Crowner sharply.

She gathered her belongings and left the hall. But the meeting was a long time breaking up, and did not break up in silence. For quite a while afterwards, through the astonished streets of Gillenham, the soul of Grandma Powley marched hilariously on.

Chapter 8

1

THE next day being Sunday, ten o'clock found Mrs. Pounce hatted and gloved in preparation for morning service. She always got ready in good time, in the hope that her church-going appearance might awake her son Nicholas, and in this case her brother-in-law Isaac also, to a sense of their civic and religious duties: for Mrs. Pounce believed that one went to church not only to please the Lord, but also to set a good example to the lower classes. She went upstairs, therefore, immediately after breakfast, and came down again, as has been said, in her hat and gloves. But the dining-room was empty save for Mrs. Leatherwright, who reported that Mr. Pounce was in his study, and Mr. Nicholas in the garden, and Miss Smith in her room. Resolutely, even hopefully—for she never learnt by experience—Mrs. Pounce set off on her missionary round.

"Isaac, dear, are you coming to church?"

"No," said the Professor.

"I think you ought to come with me, Isaac."

"Why?" asked the Professor. "Don't you know the way?"

"Of course I know the way. But I do think, dear, having taken this house, which after all is the largest in the village—you ought to set an example."

"I don't," replied Professor Pounce decisively, "rent my religion with my roof."

Mrs. Pounce felt this observation to be so unkind, so wilfully unjust to her own motives, that she could not answer it. The Professor did not seem to notice her silence, but went on ruling lines on a sheet of paper. Mrs. Pounce sighed a long, patient sigh, but he did not notice that either. She left him and went out into the garden.

"Nicholas, dear, are you coming to church?"

Nicholas, lying flat on his back in the sun, blinked up at her.

"Like this?"

His costume, consisting only of a pair of flannel trousers, was indeed unsuitable. Mrs. Pounce smiled. One line of her strategy was about to be justified.

"Of course not, darling. But there's plenty of time for you to put some clothes on."

"I haven't a clean shirt, Mother."

"But you must have! I packed you at least half a dozen!"

"I took most of 'em out again to get some books in. I've only three shirts down here, and I gave them all to Mrs. Leatherwright to wash."

"Then what are you going to put on this evening, when it gets cold?"

"My jersey," said Nicholas. "Skylark. The only one I've brought."

His mother looked down at him, frustrated. She knew that jersey well: it was navy-blue, with the name "Skylark" inscribed across the chest in a semi-circle of large red letters. Nicholas had acquired it in Cornwall off the owner of a pleasure-boat, and had enjoyed a great success with it among his Cambridge friends. . . .

"I'll come in that, if you like," he offered amiably.

Mrs. Pounce very much wished she had the strength of mind to accept. But she couldn't. She couldn't make her first appearance in a strange congregation accompanied by a son with Skylark on his chest. She had to think of the choirboys. And it was no use calling Nicholas' bluff, because she knew he wasn't bluffing. He had the strangest indifference to what really nice people thought. It was one of the traits he had brought back from the University, and one which Mrs. Pounce simply couldn't understand.

Suddenly she felt angry.

"Nicholas," she said, "if you don't want to come to church, I'd far rather you said so outright. It would be so much more manly."

"All right," agreed Nicholas. "I don't."

He smiled at her affectionately, turned over, and buried his face in the grass. Mrs. Pounce looked down at his nice bare back, already an even pinkish-brown, and felt a wave of bewilderment. For all she could learn from it, she might just as well be looking at his back as his face. She thought of his father, and her bewilderment increased.

"Oh, dear!" said Mrs. Pounce.

Nicholas turned his head.

"If you're really unhappy about it, darling, I'll wear Skylark back to front."

"No," said Mrs. Pounce. "No, dear. I'll try Carmen, and then I must be off."

She went upstairs to Carmen's room, and outside its closed door stood a moment in hesitation. She did not really want Carmen to come with her. She felt her presence would be somehow embarrassing. But she also felt that, far more than her son, far more than her brother-in-law even, it was Miss Smith who needed to be exposed to religion. She knocked.

"Who's that?" called Carmen.

"Would you like to come to church?" called back Mrs. Pounce.

"No, thanks," said Carmen.

This time Mrs. Pounce did not persist.

2

Walking through the quiet lanes, hearing the birds sing and the bells ring, Mrs. Pounce suddenly felt very happy. She had much to displease her, much to worry her; she had no one to speak to, all Nicholas' shirts were in the wash—or rather she hoped they were, as if not he was telling a lie—and her brother-in-law had been positively cruel; but none of these things now troubled Mrs. Pounce. She felt pleased and expectant; she hoped there would be a nice sermon, and good singing, but if there weren't she wouldn't really mind. She was going to church. It was the one time in her nervous, harassed, bewildered life when she felt complete self-confidence. She was performing an incontrovertibly right act. She was paying the most important of all Calls, properly dressed for the Occasion. Mrs. Pounce could never understand people who dropped familiarly in and out of churches, praying for ten minutes here and there just as they felt like it. It seemed disrespectful to her, and rather pushing. She genuinely felt that the Lord was At Home on Sundays, and that was when He wanted to see you. He had many other worlds on His hands as well as this one. Mrs. Pounce's theology was instinctive rather than reasoned, and she had never considered the question of Who dealt with her morning and evening prayers; had she done so, she would probably have visualized an Archangel secretariat, and with it have been content.

So Mrs. Pounce walked happily along, her prayer-book in her hand, half-a-crown for the collection tucked inside her glove, and her heart filled with confidence in herself and her Creator.

3

No less happy, that morning, was Professor Pounce, ambitiously blocking out the scheme of his monograph; ambitiously, because its completion depended on an intimate knowledge of the sex-life of each subject. He had ruled three columns, the first for Names and Ages, the second for Comment, the third for the results of the testing. What the Professor meant by comment may be gathered from the couple of imaginary examples he had already filled in:

Name and Age.	*Comment.*	*Result.*	*Marks.*
Mary Brown Age: 35.	Unmarried, two children.	Fell headlong.	0
Martha Jones Age: 70.	Mother Superior.	Crossed dry-shod.	100

These two examples, of course, represented the high and low limits, and were completely unambiguous. But it was just the possibility of ambiguousness which both troubled and fascinated Professor Pounce. He wrote again.

Name and Age.	*Comment.*	*Result.*	*Marks.*
Susie Smith Age: 21.	Her mother says she's a good girl.	Lost her footing.	?

Before Susie Smith the Professor sat a long while in thought. He didn't see how the thing could be proved one way or the other—unless, of course, by affidavit from the girl herself; and even he, accustomed as he was to ignore the commoner manifestations of human nature, realized that such a document, if it supported the Stone's verdict, might be difficult to obtain. There was, however, such a thing as Common Knowledge. Common Knowledge might do it. He inserted a forth column, with this heading, between "Comment" and "Result," and rather unfairly wrote in the word "Flighty." The case of Susie Smith now looked much more convincing. He crossed out "Flighty" and substituted "Receives ten shillings a week from source unknown." The case was now practically watertight. Then out of sheer fair-mindedness he filled in another line for one Hetty Cook:

He even felt she ought to have 100 plus, but since he intended to strike an average at the end, this would make things too complicated.

Name and Age.	*Comment.*	*Common Knowledge.*	*Result.*	*Marks.*
Hetty Cook Age: 26.	Married.	Husband aged 90.	Dry-shod.	100

The important thing now was to gather Common Knowledge, and here the Professor paused. He was exceptionally good at acquiring the uncommon sort, but he felt that this mere spadework could safely be left to a lesser intelligence. So he went out to look for Nicholas, whom he found trying to mix a dry Martini without any ice.

4

Nicholas needed a drink rather badly because he had just had his ears boxed by Carmen Smith. It happened in a rather interesting way.

As soon as his mother was out of the house Nicholas sat up, extracted from underneath him the paper and pencil which he had hidden at her approach, and went on with what he was doing. He was making a portrait of Carmen, from memory. It was fairly easy to produce a recognizable likeness: the thick straight fringe, the thick straight eyebrows, could not be mistaken, and by scribbling in a scarf he avoided the subtler lines of cheek and jawbone. He worked away in the happy calm of complete absorption, for he had all unwittingly discovered the only means by which Carmen's extraordinary looks could be rendered sexually innocuous. When Carmen herself came out of the house, his senses did not warn him of her presence. She came up behind him unobserved, looked over his shoulder, and only her shadow on the paper made him turn his head.

"How's that?" asked Nicholas complacently.

He expected her to be pleased and flattered; Carmen was neither of these things. Her eyes were stony, her hand whipped out, and the next moment Nicholas' right ear buzzed like a beehive.

"I say!" he protested. "What's wrong with it?"

"It's bilking," said Carmen.

Nicholas stared.

"Bilking? Who am I bilking?"

"Me," said Carmen. "I'm half-a-crown an hour. Or all day Thursdays in the Life Class if you've paid your fees for the term."

"You mean," said Nicholas, as light dawned, "you're a professional model?"

"Of course I am." She seized the paper and tore it violently across.

"But how was I to know that?"

"I'm famous," said Carmen. "You ask your uncle."

She stalked off, and Nicholas, as has been said, went in to mix himself a dry Martini.

5

"I'll have one of those too," said the Professor. "Don't overestimate your capacity, my boy, because this evening—"

"Uncle Isaac," interrupted Nicholas, "I didn't know Carmen was a model."

Rather impatiently, the Professor informed him that Carmen was a very famous model indeed. She was the Demeter of the last year's Academy, the Niobe of the Regent's Park fountain, the Modern Madonna whose exhibition had brought in the police. . . .

"Then what's she doing here?" asked Nicholas, point-blank.

"She always takes a holiday in the summer," replied Professor Pounce vaguely.

"But aren't you paying her?"

"Not for posing, my dear boy. She's very snobbish. She poses only for RA.'s, and I believe the London School—and, of course, for one or two prominent rebels."

"How did you come across her, sir?"

"In a pub," said the Professor. "As I was just about to say, I want you to patronize the public-house here, The Grapes, this evening, for as long as may seem useful."

Nicholas looked at his uncle suspiciously.

"In what way useful, sir?"

"I want you to gather Common Knowledge. I believe Sunday evening is a very good time."

Nicholas looked at his uncle more suspiciously than ever. The old boy wasn't changing the subject, he had a definite aim.

"What sort of common knowledge? To do with the Stone?"

"Naturally. I want you to get a rough general idea as to which of the girls here are accepted as being virgins, and which, if married, are accepted as being faithful to their husbands. With the reasons, if possible—and you might make a note, in each case, of the source of information."

"Not on your life," said Nicholas promptly.

"Do it delicately, of course," added Professor Pounce, apparently not hearing him.

Nicholas gulped down his drink and poured out another.

"You can't, sir. You can't do a thing like that delicately. And I'm damned if I'm going to go asking questions about the love-life of Gillenham in a public bar."

His uncle looked at him with patience.

"I don't wish you to ask questions. I merely want you to keep your ears open, and possibly guide the conversation into the appropriate channel."

Nicholas knocked back his drink, and poured out a third, and knocked that back as well.

"Uncle Isaac," he said clearly, "don't you think you're rather a cad?"

"No," replied the Professor positively.

"Well, I do," said Nicholas. "You'd not only kiss and tell, you'd seduce and publish."

"I should do nothing of the sort," retorted the Professor. "I've never seduced a woman in my life, and I've never kissed a woman except my mother."

This obviously truthful statement gave Nicholas a moment's pause. He changed his ground.

"I think that's worse," he said. "You won't even do the work yourself. Uncle Isaac, I think that's terrible."

The Professor gave him a searching look, and carefully replaced the corks in the bottles of gin and vermouth.

"You have no sense of economy," he remarked unexpectedly. "I don't desire to find evidences of unchastity, but if such evidence exists, far better it should serve some useful purpose than go to waste. I hold no brief for the practice of seduction, in fact I deplore it; but if a young woman has been seduced already, why shouldn't I make use of the fact for my monograph? Employing, of course, a fictitious name for the village, and a letter of the alphabet for that of the subject?"

Nicholas really couldn't see why not.

"Your whole trouble," continued the Professor, "is that you have ignored one operative word: delicately. Crudely to question a yokel about his amours, crudely to encourage him (as you put it) to tell of his kisses, would be very indelicate indeed. If you can't perform the task with delicacy, leave it alone, and I will undertake it myself."

Gin and apprehension combined made Nicholas feel suddenly ill.

"Please don't, Uncle Isaac! Please don't think of it!"

"Well, it's either you or I," pointed out the Professor. "Your mother hasn't enough *nous*. There's Carmen, of course—"

Nicholas gulped. At whatever cost, Carmen must be kept out of it.

"If you don't expect me to ask questions, sir—"

"Haven't I said I don't?"

"If you just want me to go and hang about the village a bit, I—I'll take it on."

"Good," said the Professor cheerfully. "I'm glad you've seen reason." He uncorked the bottles and refilled his glass, not, however, offering any to Nicholas. He seemed to have taken to gin and French quite surprisingly, for when he returned to his study he carried both bottles with him, and Nicholas distinctly heard the corner cupboard being opened, and closed, and then locked up.

6

Of all the hours in the week seven o'clock on Sunday evening had, in Gillenham, the most special character; for it was the hour when the youth and beauty of the village, attired as to the male portion in reach-me-down suits and cloth caps, as to the female in artificial silk frocks and straw hats, came out in search of hebdomadal romance. Professor Pounce had chosen well.

The opening stages of the proceedings were governed by a rigid code: first the youths appeared, Jack Thirkettle and Jack Uffley and the two Fletchers, and the day-men from Vander's and Old Farm, and formed little groups at the street corner and outside the door of The Grapes. (Their seniors were all within, at the bar.) They stood apparently unexpectant—smoking, shuffling their feet, exchanging desultory remarks—for about a quarter of an hour. They were the quarry rather than the hunters. At seven-fifteen the first frocks hove into sight as Mabel and Violet Brain appeared on Bowen's Bridge. This was not due to any forwardness on the part of the Brain sisters; they had to walk in from Vander's Farm; from the bridge to The Grapes took five minutes, and they knew that by the time they arrived they would have plenty of female support.

At seven-twenty, every girl in the village was out parading.

They walked in pairs, for the sake of modesty, and giggled, to attract attention.

There were, however, several accepted ways of losing one's companion, such as finding a stone in one's shoe opposite The Grapes, or dropping one's bag at the street corner; and presently the caps were mingling with the straw hats, the groups were enlarged and enlivened by passages of traditional wit, and then all at once, like a figure in a country dance, the street was again filled with couples. But this time the pairs walked lad and lass, and the parade-ground was extended from the village to the fields beyond. The hedges swallowed them up; Gillenham was a desert until nine forty-five; at which hour all courting had to cease because The Grapes shut at ten, and it was unthought-of to forgo one's last Sunday pint for the sake of fifteen minutes more of female society.

Such was the usual procedure, designed, as will have been seen, for masculine convenience; such the spectacle to which Nicholas, hanging sheepishly about the street, would normally have been treated; but on this particular Sunday the procedure was varied. The youths came out, the maidens duly appeared, but there was no mingling; and as each lad tried to cut out and carry off his lass he found himself foiled. The single copy of Professor Pounce's questionnaire preserved by the girl Sally had done its work. Every young woman in the village had seen it, Mabel Brain had even copied it out, and the shadow of the Government—visualized by many as a stalwart Policewoman—invisibly chaperoned their steps. As a result, the girls stuck together. They none of them wanted a walk. They wanted to stay there, in full view, under their mothers' windows. . . .

But they giggled as much as ever.

Indeed, as the chagrin of their swains became apparent, they giggled rather more. The Professor's questionnaire had done several unexpected things, and one of them was to promote a hitherto impossible female trade unionism. Before, coquetry had been almost unknown, because there were too many girls who would go with the first lad who asked them, and to make oneself difficult might be to find oneself left; now they were all in the same boat, and they discovered unsuspected advantages. After prolonged consultation Violet Brain agreed to take a turn round the houses with Jack Uffley, and he got her as far as Bowen's Spinney—only to discover Joy and Martha Fox tagging along behind. They tagged, giggling and nudging, all round the spinney, and Violet, instead of giving them a piece of her mind, actually joined in their foolishness over her shoulder, so that Jack Uffley received the impression that they were giggling at him. It was all most surprising and unsatisfactory. Nor did Jack's fellows fare any better; the two Fletchers, acknowledged lady-killers, never even got away from their station outside The Grapes. The girls paraded up and down, pleased as plums; the swains stood angry and bewildered; altogether, it was the queerest Sunday evening Gillenham had ever seen.

7

"It's all right, Uncle Isaac," reported Nicholas cheerfully. "You can go straight ahead."

The Professor, who had been eagerly awaiting his nephew's return on the front lawn, cocked an eyebrow.

"Of course I'm going ahead," he said. "What do you mean?"

"I mean you won't find any funny business in Gillenham, sir. It's positively Spanish. The girls won't even speak to a man unless they've two chaperons and a witness. They were all out in their Sunday best, and they never even left the main street."

The Professor's delight at this good news was not as apparent as might have been expected.

"Did you go into The Grapes?" he asked.

"I did," said Nicholas. "I went in when the rest of them did, and listened with all my ears. But I didn't hear anything because there wasn't anything to hear. They were the most speechless crowd I've ever struck."

"Extraordinary!" said Professor Pounce.

CHAPTER 9

1

NEXT morning Professor Pounce for some reason came down to breakfast in a very bad humour. His sister-in-law looked at him apprehensively, and wished the papers arrived sooner. Given a good substantial newspaper, such as the *Times*, a man could make it into a sort of tent, and thus avoid too early contact with his nearest and dearest. Nicholas wished that they followed the more civilized habit of breakfasting separately, but this was considered too much trouble for Mrs. Leatherwright. They all sat down rather glum, and the Professor stirred his porridge and reached for the cream-jug. It was empty.

"No cream," he said. "Maud, where's the cream?"

"It hasn't come, dear," said Mrs. Pounce nervously.

"Then pass me the milk."

"The milk hasn't come either, dear."

"Why hasn't it come?"

"I don't know," said Mrs. Pounce. "It just hasn't."

The Professor pushed back his chair and looked at her with restraint.

"Nor has the butter," added Mrs. Pounce, making a clean breast of it. "And it's no use asking me why, Isaac, because I don't know. I expect Mrs. Pye just forgot."

Nicholas sat up.

"Do we get it from Vander's Farm?"

"Regularly, dear. Mrs. Pye sends round every morning—milk and cream and butter and eggs. We've still got two eggs. I'll walk across after breakfast and speak to her about it."

"Nonsense!" snapped the Professor. "Nicholas will walk across now, and bring the stuff back with him. I insist on starting the day with a civilized meal."

Unwillingly Nicholas rose. He dared not protest, lest his uncle should hit on the idea of sending Carmen instead; but it was with extremely reluctant feet that he followed the field-path to Vander's. The basket on his arm, containing two empty jugs and a dish for the butter—the whole neatly covered with a white napkin—lent him a Red-Riding-Hood look of which he was uneasily aware. He felt pretty sure that the Wolf was before him. He very much hoped Mrs. Pye would not be up, but from all he knew of her character this seemed most improbable, nor could he make up his mind whether she were less likely to be in the house or the yard. He decided to try the yard first, and there had the good fortune to encounter Mabel Brain crossing from byre to back-door.

"Good morning," said Nicholas, quite boldly. "I've come for our milk and cream and butter and eggs."

Mabel giggled. She always giggled when suddenly addressed, but Nicholas did not know this, and felt slightly less bold than before.

"For the Old Manor," he added. "You forgot to deliver them."

He produced his two jugs. But Mabel backed away.

"You better see missus," she said firmly.

"I don't want to see missus," said Nicholas. "Just fill these jugs like a good girl, and give me a dozen eggs and two pounds of butter—"

In the back of the farmhouse a sash was flung up, and in the open window appeared the mobled head of Mrs. Pye. With another giggle Mabel fled. Nicholas stood his ground, gaping up as Mrs. Pye gazed down. Time seemed to pass over them as it passed over the Statue and the Bust. Then the lips of the Bust monosyllabically moved.

"Well?"

Nicholas jumped. The jugs clashed together.

"I've come," he repeated, "for our milk and cream and butter and eggs . . ."

"There aren't none," said Mrs. Pye.

Behind the byre wall a cow lowed. From the coops beyond came a triumphant clucking of hens. The whole place was pullulating with potential eggs and butter and cream and milk.

"Really," said Nicholas, "I can hardly believe that. . . ."

"Try," said Mrs. Pye.

A hen clucked again. He instinctively turned towards the sound.

"Set one foot near my coops," said Mrs. Pye, "and I'll have you up for trespass. There's no eggs here for Old Manor, nor no milk nor butter nor cream. Nor there won't be. Good day!"

She slammed down the window and disappeared. Nicholas waited a moment longer, not so much in the hope she might relent as because he did not know what to do next. But when he did move he moved quickly. There was a rattling and a barking in one of the outhouses which unmistakably suggested a dog being let off its chain; and Nicholas did not wait to see what breed the Pyes fancied.

Five minutes later, as he was walking defeated down the lane, he came upon the neat cottage of the Tom Uffleys. There were hen-coops at the side, and a shed which might or might not contain a cow. With renascent hope Nicholas went up the path and knocked at the door. It was opened by Mrs. Tom.

"Good morning," said Nicholas. "I wonder whether you could let me have any milk or butter—" The words were beginning to sound like the chorus of a song. "Or eggs or cream?"

Mrs. Tom hesitated.

"You'll be from Old Manor?"

"That's right," Nicholas agreed. "We happen to have run out of butter and milk—"

"We've none here," said Mrs. Tom.

Nicholas, glancing over her shoulder into the room beyond, distinctly saw on the dresser a bowl containing eggs. He was struck by a sudden and most unpleasant idea.

"Where does your husband work?" he asked.

"At Vander's. He's Mr. Pye's cowman."

"Thank you," said Nicholas. "Good-bye."

2

After his mutilated breakfast the Professor's humour was even worse than before, nor did Nicholas feel particularly sunny. He simply could not get his uncle to grasp the unpalatable fact that a scientific investigation into a renascent Norse legend might have a direct effect on the supply of milk and cream and butter and eggs.

"I've never heard anything so preposterous!" cried the Professor.

"I dare say not," admitted Nicholas wearily, "but it's a fact all the same. Mrs. Pye has given the word, and none of their people will supply us."

The Professor reflected. He seemed unusually ready to accept, if he could not understand, the situation. The next moment Nicholas saw why.

"After all." said Professor Pounce, "the inconvenience is but a trifling one. You can walk into the village each day before breakfast, and fetch the comestibles from there. The stroll will be very pleasant."

"Suppose it rains," objected Nicholas.

"Then instead of strolling, you will walk at a brisk pace. You will lift your feet more smartly, and place them one before the other in an accelerated rhythm, and thus diminish the period of your exposure to the elements. I suppose you do know rain when you see it? It isn't something you've just heard of?"

Nicholas went out to the summer-house and swore.

3

In the parlour at Vander's Farm Mrs. Pye stood thinking about sin. She had gone down from her encounter with Nicholas, filled with the energy of triumph, to conduct a lightning inspection of every room; now she had been standing almost an hour, rapt in contemplation, while the work of the house and yard slowly ran down and stopped; for these trances of Mrs. Pye's were well known. They afforded a welcome respite, a holiday from her ceaseless supervision. Whoever first caught sight of the stiff unmoving figure hastened to spread the news; and a little tide of gossip and easiness began to spread through the house.

"Missus is off again!" reported Violet Brain, putting her head through the wash-house door. "There's George in the yard, see will he help hang the sheets. . . ."

Mrs. Pye stood unmoving. Her eyes were fixed on a glass jar filled with variegated sand from the Isle of Wight; but she did not see it. At the back of her mind was a dim consciousness of the passage of time; she thrust it down. She was living, more vividly and intensely than any passage of daily life, her mystic role of Denunciatrix. It was a curious and elaborate exercise of the imagination: first she built up the images of lust and luxury, then she stepped in and destroyed them. She created the chamber of Jezebel, furnishing it, from the engravings in an old Bible, with cushions and carpets, and great jars spilling wine, and platters of heavy fruit, and the shameless woman herself half-naked under the eyes of her paramour; and there were more shameless women dancing to strange music, and men who caught at them as they passed, ripping the thin veils and laughing in their drunkenness. And Jezebel stood up, and cast her last garment from her, and began to dance also, and her paramour put out his hand to trip her, and then—and then Mrs. Pye strode in, and the music stopped, and they all cowered away while Mrs. Pye lashed them with her tongue and spurned the wine-pots with her foot, and Jezebel tried to hide herself. And Mrs. Pye dipped her finger in the spilth of the wine and wrote on the wall with it: MENE, MENE, TEKEL, UPHARSIN; and they all abased themselves before her, pleading in terror for forgiveness. . . .

Mrs. Pye drew a long shuddering breath. The jar of variegated sand came suddenly into focus before her eyes. She picked it up, fingered it automatically for dust, and finding it clean set it back in its place. That was what she had come into the parlour to do. Now she felt oddly tired. It took all her strength to go out into the pasture, and there berate the girls for wasting George's time.

4

The summer-house, with its associations both of Carmen and (through the Bluebell Court) of Miss Hyatt, recalled to Nicholas his design of getting to know all about women. He was glad to think of something which concerned only himself; he felt an urgent need to live his own life for a bit—a proceeding unexpectedly difficult in a household which included Professor Pounce.

He started off by thinking about Carmen Smith; but even here his uncle horned in. The connection between Carmen and the Professor was still wrapped in mystery; all Nicholas knew for certain was that they had met in a pub. It seemed as though all Carmen's social contacts were so formed: she had landed Mr. Pye in a pub, and the man who knew about falling in love, and now the Professor; and each of the three had apparently been able, as Nicholas had not, to reach some sort of understanding with the wench. The uneasy suspicion that she was in some way beyond him recurred; unfortunately, he was now more fascinated by her than ever. She was a model; she knew the *vie de bohème* from the inside, and with the *vie de bohème* Nicholas passionately desired to become familiar. He had spent much of the previous afternoon (a handsome apology offered and accepted) in eager questioning; but on Carmen's beautiful lips tales of the *vie de bohème* took on a surprising dullness. She knew nothing of art save its price list. She liked sculpture best because sculptors booked you for a good long time, three months, maybe, and you knew where you were. She looked down on the Chelsea school because so few of the studios there were centrally heated. If she posed in the open air, she charged double. . . .

She liked Professor Pounce because he paid her in advance. But she didn't say what for.

Altogether, she was a very uneasy subject of contemplation for a romantic young man in a summerhouse, and with a violent effort of the will Nicholas switched his thoughts to Mildred Hyatt. There was fortunately as yet no link between Miss Hyatt and the Professor, and her image was for that reason at least inoffensive. After about half an hour it became even stimulating: Nicholas decided that though he wasn't at all in love with her—which made the whole project somehow more sophisticated, and consequently more pleasing—she was really quite attractive, and quite worthy of being made love to. He would have gone round and started in at once, except for the earliness of the hour: eleven o'clock, and on a Monday morning, was no time to embark on amorous adventure. A phrase from the French occurred to his mind: *"Cinq à six, l'heure des petites liaisons"*; it seemed to express just what he wanted. With some slight difficulty, but with great sophistication, he went on thinking about Miss Hyatt in French. *Elle était vraiment très gentille; on lui ferait un petit brin de cour, et on prendrait ce qu'on offraient les dieux. . . .* (Or should it be *offreraient*?) *Elle avait de très jolies yeux, une jolie petite figure—non, taille—elle méritait bien un peu d'attention. . . .*

Where was now the moral, the virtuous Nicholas who only twenty-four hours earlier had called his old uncle a cad? Gone with the wind—which was the title of the book Miss Hyatt put down as she saw him coming up the path to Rose Cottage in the late afternoon.

5

The hour was nearer six than five, for tea at the Old Manor had been delayed, and also it was raining. Nicholas at first thought he would wait for a finer day, then realized that with the evenings so long and light an overcast sky was rather an asset, affording a good excuse to draw the curtains against the weather. He naturally did not make this suggestion at once, but waited till Miss Hyatt had seen and admired his verses about the fairy chimes, and had also played him a fragment of her *Symphonie Moderne*. To Nicholas it did not sound like anything on earth, modern or otherwise, but he made without difficulty several vague complimentary remarks. Mildred Hyatt seemed very glad to see him.

"With my work, I never feel in the least *lonely*," she explained, "but it's nice to talk to someone who understands."

"I know," said Nicholas, understanding. "Isn't it a filthy day?" He looked towards the window, against which the rain was driving with renewed force. "Let's draw the curtains and shut it out."

"The lamp's gone wrong," said Mildred.

"I'll put it right for you," said Nicholas insincerely. But to his annoyance, when the curtains were drawn, she actually produced the thing, a large Victorian contraption smelling of cheap oil. It was, however, perfectly easy for Nicholas to fix it so that it wouldn't light at all, and as he gave it back to Miss Hyatt their hands definitely met. Miss Hyatt jumped.

"You'll want to wash," she said, rather nervously. "You can use the kitchen, if you like . . ."

"What about your landlady?"

"She won't mind. She's out."

This useful piece of information sent Nicholas to the sink with a light heart, and when he returned the very fact of his coming in from the kitchen made them feel suddenly intimate. Miss Hyatt had poured out two glasses of a rich brown sherry, and drinking together in the gloom made them feel more intimate still. It was time for action. Nicholas got up from his chair and replaced his glass on the table and sat down again on the sofa, beside Mildred. After a few moments he slid his arm along the horsehair-covered back, and his hand came in contact with Mildred's shoulder. She was wearing an orange polo-jersey, very agreeable to the touch. Nicholas gently stroked it.

"Have you read *Gone With the Wind*?" asked Miss Hyatt, in a detached but slightly breathless voice.

"No," said Nicholas. She hadn't moved away, so he tightened his hold, pulling her a little towards him.

"It's awfully good. It's all about the American Civil War."

"Is it?" said Nicholas. He wished he had put out his cigarette before sitting down, for the stub was burning his fingers. Risking a long shot, he chucked it towards the grate, and the manoeuvre was doubly successful, for not only did the butt land safely within the fender, but the jerk brought Miss Hyatt's head finally down upon his chest.

"It tells you all about Atlanta," she continued, from this new position, "and all about the Democrats and Carpetbaggers and people. Though I don't think that part's so interesting as the first."

"I haven't read it," said Nicholas, with his cheek on her hair. It was nice hair, soft and well-kept, and it wasn't full of bobby-pins or other man-traps. He drew his cheek softly up and down; and in an absent-minded sort of way, as though too much absorbed in the intellectual side of their converse to notice any change in its physical circumstances, Miss Hyatt settled farther into his arms.

"There's a wonderful bit about a retreat . . ."

For some minutes Nicholas continued happily enough to kiss Miss Hyatt's hair while Miss Hyatt continued to recapitulate the saga of Scarlett O'Hara. But *Gone With the Wind* is a long work, and even though he had never read it Nicholas had often eyed its bulk upon the bookstalls. The polo-jersey, moreover, was a baffling garment. Miss Hyatt had knitted it herself, and put plenty of wool into it, and it did not so much cling as swaddle.

"Aren't you fearfully hot?" asked Nicholas.

Miss Hyatt did not interrupt her résumé to answer but she emitted a short, stifled sigh. To the account of Rhett Butler's blockade-running Nicholas carefully removed the polo-jersey. Just as it came over her head Miss Hyatt's voice suddenly rose an octave, but whether from emotion, or from the desire to make herself heard, Nicholas could not honestly tell. In any case, the account was becoming a mere babble, the words ran together, all sense was lost, and what might have happened neither of them knew, when at that moment, in the depths of the sofa, a spring twanged.

It twanged on the precise note of B flat.

"Oh, damn!" said Nicholas.

He released Miss Hyatt as though she had been a hot potato. It was ungallant, it was unpardonable, but he could not help it. The painful memory that had haunted him for months was like a douche of cold water.

"What is it?" whispered Miss Hyatt.

"Someone coming," muttered Nicholas resourcefully. "I'd better go."

There was a hasty soft scuffling—how all the sounds recurred!—and when Nicholas rapidly embraced her at the door his hands once more touched thick wool.

"Oh, *darling*," murmured Miss Hyatt.

Nicholas, as has been said, possessed a very accurate ear. Beneath the fervour of her tone he detected—how *all* the sounds recurred!—a faint, an almost imperceptible note of relief.

"I'll see you to-morrow," he promised insincerely; and went very quickly out into the rain.

6

Far away on the other side of Ipswich three persons who have very little to do with this history were sitting down to dinner. They were Sir Peter Sprigg and his wife Cecile, and a Member of Parliament down for a holiday. He was a very young M.P., so young that he was still constantly looking for audiences to address. Lady Sprigg knew this, and being a kind-hearted woman and a good hostess was anxious to indulge him; her husband also was kind-hearted, but he had heard young Coulter speak in the House, and had no wish to put his neighbours to a similar ordeal. Lady Sprigg, however, was a woman of resource.

"Jimmy," she said to Mr. Coulter, "have you ever spoken at Gillenham?"

James Coulter at once put down his soup-spoon. His eye brightened. One could almost see his ears cock.

"No, I haven't," he said. "Where is it?"

"Over beyond Ipswich. It's quite a small place—"

"It's a village," put in Sir Peter bluntly. "Regular hole in the ground."

"I don't mind that," said Mr. Coulter. He didn't mind anything. He had once deputized for a lady novelist at a college literary circle. And he did so not merely from love of hearing his own voice, but from a sincere desire to benefit his hearers. He was a very good and conscientious young man.

"I'm sure they'd love to have you," continued Lady Sprigg. "It must be years and years since any one's taken any notice of them. Don't you think it's a good idea, Peter?"

Her husband, considering the comparative remoteness of Gillenham from his own estate, had begun to think it a very good idea indeed.

"Excellent," he said. "You go over, Coulter, and tell 'em about the Channel Tunnel."

Young Mr. Coulter slightly flushed. As a dressmaker, seeking originality, harks back to the bustle or the crinoline, so Coulter, seeking some distinctive label, had harked back to the Channel Tunnel. But he had come to think it a mistake.

"I'd rather speak on Decimal Coinage," he said. "I've been getting it up."

"The very thing," agreed Sir Peter heartily. "It'll be all one to—"

His wife kicked him under the table. But fortunately Mr. Coulter had not heard.

"Who's their Member?" he asked. "I don't want to poach."

"It's old Muirhead," Sir Peter told him, "and he won't care. You're both Unionists. He'll be only too glad to have some work taken off his hands. I'll phone his agent to-night, and get the whole thing fixed up."

Mr. Pomfret, the Unionist agent, seemed astonished rather than delighted by the proposal; but he made no objection, and it was thus arranged that young Mr. Coulter should go over to Gillenham on the following Wednesday week, there to address the populace on the subject of Decimal Coinage.

Chapter 10

1

The party at the Old Manor had now been installed for a full week, and Carmen and Professor Pounce were thoroughly enjoying themselves. Nicholas and his mother were not.

For Nicholas' love-life was now in a bit of a mess. The only result of his designs on Miss Hyatt was that he was extremely anxious not to meet her, and he often went as much as a mile out of his way to avoid passing Rose Cottage. On the other hand, he still wanted to kiss Carmen, and frequently managed to do so, but only at the price of continual dodging about the house and garden. He had never before noticed that his mother was so mobile. He could see her in the sitting-room, apparently settled for the morning, and five minutes later encounter her at the bottom of the lane. Five minutes after that she would be looking out of her bedroom window, which commanded a view of the entire garden. There was also the Professor to be dodged, and Mrs. Leatherwright, and the daily girl.

But what annoyed Nicholas most was the fact that Carmen gave him no help at all. He made a point of announcing his whereabouts in advance, saying, for example, that he was going to read in the orchard all afternoon, and would no one disturb him, but she never seemed to take notice. If the Professor happened to send her for a paper or a book, she came; if not, she stayed away. When she did come she always let Nicholas kiss her, but never kept the Professor waiting.

"You don't care a dam about me, do you?" Nicholas once asked angrily.

"Oh, yes!" said Carmen. "I think you're ever such a nice boy."

"If that's all," said Nicholas, more angrily still, "I don't see why you let me kiss you."

She looked surprised.

"Don't you want to kiss me?"

"You know dam well I do!"

"Well, then!" said Carmen, with an air of closing a futile discussion.

"And don't you like being kissed?" persisted Nicholas.

"Of course," said Carmen cheerfully. "So we're both happy. I don't know what you want."

The trouble was that Nicholas didn't know either. Part of him wanted a violent, crashing, body-and-soul love affair with her, and part of him was scared stiff at the very thought. He had a strong notion that taking to Carmen would be like taking to drink, and that he hadn't the head for her. He wondered what sort of man had, and found himself visualizing a sort of cross between a lion-tamer and a Channel swimmer. The manly breast covered with medals, the biceps prominent and tattooed. . . .

"What kind of men *do* you like, Carmen?"

"Gentlemen," said Carmen.

There was no doubt that she was extremely vulgar. It bothered Nicholas that he should still want to kiss her all the same.

He had other troubles as well: he now had to get up every morning at half-past six to walk into the village to be back in time for Mrs. Leatherwright to prepare breakfast. Even so, the Old Manor would have fared badly but for Mrs. Jim, for the single shop was not open at that hour, and none of the villagers had eggs or milk to spare. Mrs. Jim, however, got her supplies from the Cockbrows at Old Farm, and was willing to take in an extra ration for the Pounces. Nicholas tried fetching two dozen eggs at a time, and two quarts of milk; but in the sultry weather the milk turned, and there was nothing for it but to resume his daily trek. What made his case even harder was the fact that he himself breakfasted off toast and black coffee. It was only the Professor who sat down to porridge and cream, and tea with milk, and buttered bread, and a couple of soft-boiled eggs.

2

Mrs. Pounce's trouble was simply that she had no one to speak to; and what made *her* case harder was the fact that if only she could have spoken to Mrs. Crowner, she would have been perfectly happy. Their respective social positions—one the wife of a Vicar, the other the widow of a Bank Manager—made them natural associates; they had moreover the same outlook on life, which is to say that they both avoided, wherever possible, its larger aspects, and thoroughly enjoyed its minor amenities. They could have gone shopping to Ipswich together; they could have taken tea with each other; Mrs. Pounce could have talked about her son Nicholas, and Mrs. Crowner about her daughter Bridget, who was a kindergarten mistress in London. It is quite melancholy to contemplate the hours of candid pleasure which these two ladies missed. And they missed them by so little, by so undeserved a piece of bad luck; for Mrs. Crowner, in her Christian charity, actually set out from the Vicarage to call on Mrs. Pounce.

In the normal way she would have called at once; the scandal of the Stone had determined her not to call at all; then the appearance of Mrs. Pounce at morning service made her change her mind. Discreetly observant over the edge of her hymn-book, she recognized a practised worshipper. Mrs. Pounce stood, sat and knelt without the slightest hesitation. There was also a new half-crown in the offertory. The following afternoon Mrs. Crowner put on her hat and gloves and set out for the Old Manor. Unfortunately, she met the Professor on the way.

He was sitting on a stile in Manor Lane absorbed in happy thoughts of suttee. Mrs. Crowner naturally did not know this: to all outward appearance he was innocently admiring the view. Mrs. Crowner paused; he looked so very old and gentle; perhaps some wild thought of converting him, of weaning him from his paganism, flashed through her mind. In any case, she paused.

For a wonder, the Professor recognized her. He rose, and raised his hat. Mrs. Crowner approached.

"Good afternoon," she said. "Isn't it a beautiful day?"

The Professor nodded. He was wondering whether, should convention so demand, she would agree to immolate herself upon the Vicar's pyre. He decided that she would. With a fascinating mental leap, he visualized her neck encircled and elongated by a dozen metal rings. He decided that over a woman such as Mrs. Crowner the power of convention was absolute. All these thoughts gave him a look of gentle attentiveness, which encouraged Mrs. Crowner very much.

"You're fond of Nature?" she asked hopefully.

"No," replied the Professor. "Are you?"

"Indeed I am," said Mrs. Crowner, slightly taken aback.

"I'm sorry to hear it," said Professor Pounce.

Now Mrs. Crowner ought to have left it at that and walked straight on. But she didn't.

"But why?" she cried. "Surely a love of Nature—"

"Love of Nature—bunkum!" retorted the Professor rudely. "The great get-out! Dr. Johnson was wiser than he knew: Patriotism, the last refuge of the scoundrel; Love of country—that is, of the countryside, of Nature—the last refuge of the egoist. Show me a man who wants to be alone with Nature, and I'll show you a man too selfish to get on with his fellows. He doesn't have to postpone his pleasures to the view. A tree doesn't mind how he leaves the bathroom. Daffodils don't want the wireless on when he wants to read. My dear lady, if you want to save your soul, leave Nature alone!"

Mrs. Crowner was thoroughly startled. She was also annoyed by the reference to her soul. It savoured of the Devil quoting Scripture.

"I think you're quite wrong," she said sharply. "I have lived in the country all my life, and I know from experience what a good, refining influence Nature is. People come out from the cities, worn and nervous and irritable, and after a few months close to Nature—"

"They sink back to the level of vegetables," interrupted the Professor. "I've noticed that myself. But what about the folk who live close to Nature all the year round? What about your villagers here? Do you find them particularly refined?"

Mrs. Crowner was a truthful woman. She hedged.

"I don't think many of them are really what one would call Nature-lovers at all . . ."

"Of course not!" cried the Professor joyfully. "And why? Because the Nature they're so close to is the real thing, not a pretty picture on a grocer's calendar. *They* have to postpone their pleasures all right. They have to rise at uncomfortably early hours, and go out in inclement weather, and work extra time when they don't want to. They wrestle with Nature, drive her like a horse. And as a result they're not refined, but brutalized. Take a shepherd, for example—"

"The lambs—!" ejaculated Mrs. Crowner.

"Very pretty little creatures. I dare say you derive a certain pleasure from looking at them. I can't see how you derive refinement, though I don't say it's impossible. But what refinement does the shepherd derive from rubbing blue dye on a ram's belly?"

Mrs. Crowner gasped.

*"Oh," she murmured. "I didn't know . . ."

"I thought not," said the Professor happily. "The reason, of course—"

But Mrs. Crowner did not wait to hear it. She turned her back on him and hurried away. She hurried back to the Vicarage, away from the Old Manor. She never tried to call on Mrs. Pounce again.

Even this abortive gesture of courtesy might have brought that poor lady some comfort had her brother-in-law thought to mention it; but he did not. The whole incident, though it made him late for tea, which in turn made Nicholas late in calling on Miss Hyatt, passed at once and completely from the Professor's active mind.

3

Professor Pounce, absorbed in his work, was very happy. True, the Parish Registers, to which he gained access by giving Mr. Noah Uffley (churchwarden) a present of five shillings, showed no record of any Blodgett or Blodger, nor did the name appear on any tombstone; but the Professor was prepared for set-backs. They rather added to the pleasure of the chase. Professor Pounce was very happy indeed.

So also, though in a different way, was Carmen Smith. She had met Mr. Pyce on Saturday night, and on Sunday night, in Vander's great barn, and intended to meet him many times more. Their encounters were wordless and entirely satisfying. For many years after she remembered the smell of hay and dry clover, and the feel of dew on her bare feet, and the sky through the half-door.

CHAPTER 11

1

NOW when Nicholas saw young Arthur on Saturday, young Arthur promised to perform the Stonelifting operation on Monday; but on Monday Nicholas, preoccupied with his design on Miss Hyatt, forgot all about it, and so apparently did young Arthur. On Tuesday morning Professor Pounce, paying a second call on Mrs. Ada Thirkettle, found the Stone still in place, and returned to the Old Manor in a very unpleasant frame of mind.

"I suppose you are aware," he said to Nicholas, "that the University term recommences in October?"

"Yes, Uncle Isaac," said Nicholas incautiously. "And that I have not the faculty of being in two places at once?"

"Of course not, Uncle Isaac. . . ."

"And isn't there something you can do," continued the Professor patiently, "which will render the lack of that faculty unimportant?"

Nicholas flushed.

"If you mean about getting up the Stone, sir—"

"I do indeed," said the Professor, with insulting approval. "You've grasped it at last. Please finish the business this afternoon."

Nicholas then went down to the village to take it out of young Arthur. But he had not his uncle's technique, and the wheelwright's noble sorrow was disarming. Young Arthur was quite certain he had said Tuesday, and supported this erroneous conviction with such eloquence that Nicholas himself wavered. But he stood over young Arthur while the latter gathered together his tools, and exchanged the sack he wore as an apron for another apron made of a sack, and ran a comb through his hair, and put on a pair of boots, and for some reason deposited the sum of two-and-elevenpence on the corner of the chimney-piece. (Nicholas nearly asked him whether he weren't going to make his will. The Professor would undoubtedly have done so.) All these preparations, carried out in very slow motion, lent the undertaking a great air of solemnity; but at last young Arthur was ready (lacking only a brandy-keg tied round his neck), and together they set out.

Young Arthur's was an extraordinary personality. Irritated as he was, Nicholas could not help feeling proud to be seen with him. To walk beside him was like walking in a procession. He ought to have been a Lord Mayor at least.

"Where," asked young Arthur, as they halted at Mrs. Thirkettle's door, "do you want her put?"

Nicholas hesitated. He felt that for thirty shillings he should get as much labour out of young Arthur as possible; and it would save considerable trouble if the Stone were dumped straight back into Bowen's brook. But he did not know, as his uncle undoubtedly did, the exact, the necessary spot.

"How long will you be?" he asked.

"'Bout an hour," said the wheelwright regretfully. But he did not seem to regret the length of this period, rather he regretted its brevity, as though it were beneath his dignity to take on any job lasting less than a year.

"I'll come back," said Nicholas.

2

It was most unexpected, but on that return journey—after he had been back to the Old Manor, and found Professor Pounce, and been shown the exact spot in Bowen's brook where the Stone should be replaced—Nicholas fell in love.

It was very unexpected indeed. He considered himself to be in love already, with Carmen Smith. The company of his uncle, who had insisted on returning with him to Mrs. Thirkettle's, rendered him (or so one would have thought) peculiarly unsusceptible to any tender emotion. His heart was doubly armoured by a prior infatuation and by a temporary sulkiness. But no armour availed him. He was for it again.

"What a very beautiful young woman," observed Professor Pounce.

Nicholas looked gloomily round. Standing at the Vicarage gate was a girl with fair hair. She was beautiful. She was like all the fair young girls since the world began.

"Really remarkable," murmured the Professor. "She must be Miss Crowner, though it is hard to credit."

Nicholas said nothing. They were now only a few yards away, and he saw that her eyes were grey and kind, and her hands slim and sunburned. She stood very straight, but easily, looking out on the world and enjoying it.

"Good morning, my dear," said Professor Pounce.

The girl smiled at him. She also smiled at Nicholas.

"I believe you must be Miss Crowner," continued the Professor. "I am Professor Pounce, a very respectable person, although your mother may not think so. We shall always be very pleased to see you at the Old Manor whenever you can come."

If the impetuosity of this address startled Nicholas, it did not seem to startle Bridget Crowner. She went on smiling amiably.

"Should you ever care to go for a walk," continued Professor Pounce, "I shall always be at your service. You must also borrow books. If you like to play deck-tennis, there is a cord upon the lawn. Though my nephew here would probably give you a better game than I should."

"I expect you're quite good enough for me," said Miss Crowner.

"Splendid!" said the Professor. "In that case we might also make an appropriate hole and try some putting. I hope, my dear, you have plenty of leisure?"

"Plenty," agreed Miss Crowner. "I'm here for my holiday—that is, for a part of it."

"For how long a part?"

"A week."

"Then we must lose no time. Can you come round this afternoon?"

She shook her lovely head.

"Not this afternoon. It's my first day at home."

"Then come to-morrow. At any rate, come as soon as you can. If they say I'm in my study, don't hesitate to disturb me. And if your mother raises any objection, tell her to consider it as a mission to the heathen. Now we mustn't keep you. *Au revoir*, my dear," said Professor Pounce.

She went up the path; the Professor waited until she reached the door, beaming after her in what Nicholas could not help feeling was a slightly ridiculous manner. He felt his uncle had made rather an exhibition of both of them.

"Well, *you* didn't have much to say for yourself," remarked the Professor, as they walked on.

The unfairness of this observation struck Nicholas so forcibly that he made no reply.

"If I'd been your age," continued Professor Pounce, "I wouldn't have let my old uncle make all the running. If I'd been your age—"

"I hardly see what more *you* could have done," countered Nicholas, "if you'd been half my age."

"That would make me eleven," mused the Professor. "Oh, if I'd been eleven, of course, I should simply have asked her for a kiss—and she'd no doubt have given it me."

Nicholas looked at his uncle with apprehension. He couldn't think what had come over the old boy. He was behaving exactly as though he had fallen in love at first sight, and since this was what Nicholas had done himself, he naturally resented it.

"It's a great thing to be old," said the Professor.

"If you mean, sir," agreed Nicholas spitefully, "that it gives one the right to thrust oneself upon a complete stranger—"

"Thrust oneself? Who's been thrusting themselves?"

"You have," said Nicholas.

"Not at all," retorted the Professor. "I merely, having regard to the shortness of Miss Crowner's stay here, lost no time in making the position clear. Before the beautiful and the evanescent one shouldn't waste time. My forwardness—for as such I see you choose to regard it—was actually a very high compliment. Fortunately Miss Crowner has more intelligence than you have."

"All right," said Nicholas. "We'll see whether she turns up."

"I have no doubt she will. I dare say," added the Professor complacently, "she will find me a very fascinating companion. The young of the male species can obviously have no novelty for her."

The second half of this remark was so just that the youthful male specimen who was Nicholas decided to let its outrageous preliminary alone. If his uncle considered himself fascinating he would very soon be disillusioned; at any rate Nicholas hoped so. For of all the one-idea'd old bores—

Nicholas paused. He had just realized that for the unprecedented space of twenty minutes his uncle had not mentioned the Stone of Chastity.

"Uncle Isaac," he said. "What about the Stone? The trial? Are you going to rope Miss Crowner in?"

Professor Pounce paused also.

"Certainly not."

"You mean she's—*hors concours*?"

"Of course. With practically every other woman breathing I would admit an element of doubt which makes such an experiment justifiable. With Miss Crowner it is not. I may add, Nicholas, that I am astounded at and displeased with you for making such a suggestion."

Nicholas moved to the other side of the road and kicked violently at a stone. His uncle's feelings again paralleled his own, and again he had somehow put himself in the wrong. His adoration of Bridget Crowner had been so instant and overwhelming that he had not been able to bring himself to speak to her; and now the Professor, who had himself approached her with a freedom little short of profane, was accusing him of a lack of respect. . . .

Misunderstood, browbeaten, desperately in love, Nicholas tramped gloomily on. Somewhere behind a hedge a cock crowed. It crowed sardonically. Nicholas felt it was crowing at him.

"If you hear the nightingale," said Professor Pounce suddenly, "you just thank God."

3

The village, as usual at noon, was empty, but Tom Thirkettle and one of the Uffleys stood looking at something outside the Post Office. They moved off as Nicholas and his uncle approached, disclosing a small placard about ten inches by twelve. Mr. Pomfret, the Unionist agent, hadn't taken much trouble: the announcement of James Coulter's impending visit was roughly inked in block letters. At 6.30 P.M. on Wednesday week, at The Grapes, Mr. James Coulter, M.P., would address Gillenham on the subject of Decimal Coinage. Chairman, Sir Peter Sprigg. Admission free.

Both Nicholas and the Professor looked at it without interest, and walked on.

4

"So the Stone enters on its third phase," observed the Professor thoughtfully. (He was old, all right: he could forget Bridget, put her out of his mind, as easily as though she were no more than some half-glimpsed, anonymous Girl Guide.) "I could have wished for some little ceremony—not a procession, exactly, but a going-before, a clearing of the way . . ."

Hardly had he uttered this wish, when it was granted. Young Arthur, tired of waiting, had come out to look for his employer; and as has been said before, the wheelwright was a procession in himself. In fact, the sight of young Arthur majestically strolling through Gillenham with the Stone of Chastity tucked under his arm was something so striking, so full of appeal both to the eye and to the imagination, that both Nicholas and his uncle involuntarily stopped dead.

"Norse blood, undoubtedly!" murmured Professor Pounce. "Nicholas, look at my moustache!"

With an effort, and in some surprise, Nicholas detached his gaze from the procession and looked as desired.

"It's all right," he said. "What about it?"

"I felt it prickle," explained the Professor. "The same sensation as when I first discovered the manuscript. As though the individual hairs were erecting themselves. Are they?"

"No," said Nicholas.

"Pity," said the Professor. "It would have made an interesting footnote. But, really—" he stared again at young Arthur, "he might be a Viking come to life. Miss Blodgett too, if you remember, was described as a strapping fair wench. I wonder!"

"Well, that's young Arthur Fox," said Nicholas. "His father looks like a tortoise."

"And his mother?"

"I don't know anything about her, sir."

"You wouldn't," said the Professor—but quite tolerantly. "We must find out."

Nicholas did not immediately suspect what was in his uncle's mind. Young Arthur was twice the Professor's size, and had muscles like footballs. It did not occur to Nicholas that the Professor would actually open the conversation by casting a doubt on the legitimacy of young Arthur's grandfather. But Professor Pounce always went straight to the point.

"Good morning," he said. "Do you by any chance know whether your great-grandmother was a Miss Blodgett?"

Young Arthur gazed down at the Professor reflectively, and slightly altered his grip on the Stone.

"Or possibly Blodger," added Professor Pounce, "for I suspect a certain corruption."

Nicholas held himself ready to spring. But young Arthur wasn't going to brain the Professor; he was merely thinking. Or rather, he was calculating.

"Mother was a Thirkettle," he offered at last. "She's dead. But Uncle's still above ground."

"Was that your uncle," asked Nicholas suddenly, "talking to me outside The Grapes?"

The big head nodded.

"I recognized the description," explained Nicholas.

This was really rather a clever remark; the phrase did indeed exactly sum up all that could be said of old Mr. Thirkettle: he was still above ground. But young Arthur, like his sire, was through with Nicholas. He had got thirty shillings out of him, and did not expect more. He kept his attention on the Professor.

"Such a powerful fine memory has Uncle Thirkettle, there's naught he's forgot since *s*'s were *ſ*s."

"I'd like a word with him," said Professor Pounce briskly. "Where is he to be found?"

The wheelwright considered.

"Maybe you might try The Grapes," he said thoughtfully. "Or maybe he's gone to his home. Or maybe he's out wandering. And maybe you wouldn't know him. . . ."

"I shouldn't," agreed the Professor. "Therefore you must accompany me. If we find Mr. Thirkettle at The Grapes, we can refresh ourselves at the same time."

The eye of young Arthur brightened. But like a fine, conscientious workman, he thought of his duty first. With his free hand he lightly tapped the Stone.

"Won't I finish with this here first, sir?"

"No, no," said Professor Pounce impatiently. "Give it to my nephew."

Still looking like a fine, conscientious workman, young Arthur very rapidly did so. The Stone was much heavier than it had looked while so lightly borne; Nicholas, attempting to hold it under one arm himself, found he had to clasp both hands beneath the edge and thrust out his stomach for balance. Even so his knees slightly gave.

"Can't you manage better than that?" enquired his uncle. "You look as though you might drop it."

Nicholas scowled. Young Arthur looked at him reprovingly.

"What shall I do with it, sir?"

"Carry it to the brook, of course," said Professor Pounce, "and wait. I shan't be long."

Nicholas staggered off.

5

Very pleasant was Bowen's brook, gently purling, green-banked, shadowed by the weather-beaten arch of the new bridge. No sweeter spot could be imagined in which to meditate upon love. Nicholas dumped his burden opposite the shallows (where a gap-toothed line of stepping-stones slightly broke the current) and gave himself up to traditional thoughts. Or rather, he did not actively think, he opened his heart and let Bridget Crowner fill it. He was in love. There was no lingering; no looking, as Carmen had described it, through the park railings: he was inside. Presently emerged pictures, panoramas; the thought of the shortness of Bridget's stay was agonizing; he overleapt it, and behold, he and she stood together on a hillside and heard cow bells; or they floated in a gondola; or they watched the moonlight on the Taj Mahal. Fortunately he did not know it: but Nicholas was never again to get so much pleasure out of foreign travel. . . .

At first he wandered up and down the bank; presently he sat. He sat down on the Stone of Chastity, at first without even noticing that he had done so. After a while he noticed, because it was very hard. Across thoughts of Bridget struck, discordantly, the thought of the Professor. Nicholas looked at his watch, and saw the time was nearly two o'clock. A pang of hunger surprised and annoyed him. Unless he hurried he would miss lunch altogether—pigeon pie and baked jam roll. Nicholas leapt to his feet, looked at the Stone, and paused. To leave that precious relic unguarded—at the mercy of Mrs. Crowner and her Boy Scouts—was an act too bold even for the boldness of hunger. His uncle would never forgive him. He looked anxiously towards the village, and wondered where the hell the Professor was.

Nicholas couldn't imagine—which was not surprising, for the Professor and old Mr. Thirkettle had gone into Ipswich, to the movies.

6

Such was the elder Thirkettle's price. Unlike his nephew, he had outlived the desire for mere cash: what he wanted was change, excitement, *joie de vivre*. He demanded to be taken to the cinema.

There was a bus at one o'clock, and the Professor and Mr. Thirkettle caught it. (It didn't matter about their dinners, explained the latter, because there was a dam great café in the picture-house.) They entered the auditorium just in time for the main attraction, a highly sophisticated comedy of New York life, which Mr. Thirkettle appeared to relish very much indeed. He took his boots off, and his feet smelt. The comedy was followed by a travelogue, by a cartoon, and by a news-reel, which in turn (so far as the Professor and Mr. Thirkettle were concerned) was followed by the comedy.

None of this troubled Professor Pounce. The pictures didn't trouble him because he simply absented his mind and thought about Polynesian tabus, nor did it trouble him that an usherette kept coming and spraying them with scent. He realized that his companion could not be hurried. Half-way through the second showing of the comedy the usherette returned, bringing with her a commissionaire—her aim evidently to eject them; but Mr. Thirkettle's tortoiselike appearance gave her pause. It was so impossible to tell whether he were alive or dead. She flashed her torch on Professor Pounce, who immediately feigned a like syncope; and the girl went away.

7

Nicholas, having missed his lunch, got his tea by hailing a passing urchin and sending him to the Old Manor with a note. (The urchin was a Boy Scout in mufti, and this was his good deed for the day. Mrs. Crowner would have been very much annoyed.) With the basket and thermos came Mrs. Pounce, much fluttered by the absence of her menfolk. Nicholas crudely and ill-naturedly suggested that his uncle was probably lying intoxicated in a ditch, and offered, if his mother would relieve guard over the Stone, to go in search of him; but this Mrs. Pounce refused. She refused so promptly, with such unnatural firmness, that Nicholas was visited by an odd suspicion.

Experimentally, he rose and offered her his seat. Mrs. Pounce at once backed away.

"Nicholas," she said nervously, "Nicholas—do *you* think there's anything in it?"

Nicholas was in a most unfilial mood.

"Certainly I do," he said firmly.

"But—but that would be magic!"

"So is wireless magic, to some people . . ."

Mrs. Pounce was one of them. She had only just learnt to trust the telephone. She looked uneasily at the Stone, and retreated still farther. Her expression was half-fascinated, half-alarmed. For a full minute she stood gazing; then, without another word, she fled.

Nicholas sat down again, and ate his tea.

8

For another half-hour Mr. Thirkettle sat. He was waiting for the seduction scene. The heroine saved her virtue, but lost Mr. Thirkettle's attention. He stooped down and felt for his boots.

It was now the Professor's innings. With a firm hand he piloted Mr. Thirkettle to a far corner of the dam great café and ordered him a double brandy. The café was not licensed, but again Mr. Thirkettle's appearance came in handy. No one wanted him to die on the premises. The manager opened the first-aid cupboard and produced a whole flask.

"Now, then!" said Professor Pounce.

Mr. Thirkettle was not ungrateful. He also possessed remarkable stamina. When at last he spoke, he spoke for nearly two hours. At the end of that time Professor Pounce knew as much about the inside history of Gillenham as did the Recording Angel—or possibly a little more.

9

"Nicholas, *dear*!" said Mrs. Pounce.

Such is the power of maternal love that she had again ventured forth, and at nine o'clock, into what she evidently considered the dangerous proximity of the Stone. But she kept a fair distance away.

"It's getting dark!" said Mrs. Pounce.

"You'd better send out *Anna Karenina* and a flashlight," replied her son stoically.

"But you can't stay here all night, darling! I'm sure your uncle wouldn't wish it!"

"You bet he would," said Nicholas. "Isn't he back yet?"

"No, he isn't," said Mrs. Pounce unhappily. "It's most odd, I really can't understand it, but I heard at the Post Office that he took the Ipswich bus. And really, Nicholas, I will not be left all alone by myself in that great old house all night without any one at all."

"You've got Carmen."

"I mean without a man. Nicholas, you must come home at once!"

Nicholas was not unwilling to do so. He was cold and cramped, besides being very bored, and the prospect of spending an entire night sitting on the Stone was not at all attractive.

"All right," he said. "I'd better cart this thing along with me."

"You'll do no such thing!" cried Mrs. Pounce. "I won't have it in the house!"

"I'll dump it in the garden."

"You'll do nothing of the sort. You'll leave it where it is!"

This strange, this unexampled firmness put Nicholas in something of a dilemma. He couldn't take the Stone with him, he couldn't leave it where it was, he couldn't abandon a widowed mother. He wondered if there were anywhere where he could procure a large dog: a really large dog, chained to the Stone, might satisfy even Professor Pounce. But the only large dog he knew of was the Pyes'. He thought of camouflage, of a covering of branches; then he remembered that the quicken bough, especially of Oak, Ash, or Thorn, was said to possess certain magical properties of its own: in combination with the Stone of Chastity, what powerful, what unimagined spells might not be thus unleashed? It must be remembered that it was by now nearly dark; in the thickening gloom the Stone all at once looked much larger. A bat flickered suddenly by, and both Nicholas and his mother jumped.

"Put a wastepaper-basket over it," whispered Mrs. Pounce.

"Too conspicuous," said Nicholas—also in a low voice. "It might attract attention."

"A box, then. There's an old sugar-box in the shed . . ."

This seemed to Nicholas rather a sound idea. With many a backward glance he accompanied his mother home, found the box, and hastened back with it to the banks of Bowen's brook. It fitted very neatly; but as he popped it over the Stone he felt a slight pang of apprehension, as though he were offering that inanimate object some indignity. The sugar-box had SWIFTS FOR SWEETIES written large across the sides. . . .

Nicholas rammed it down and hurried away. It was now very late indeed.

10

It was even later when the Professor and Mr. Thirkettle returned. It was nearly midnight. But they came back in style, in a hired car with a chauffeur; for they had missed the last bus. They missed it by several hours, owing to the fact that they had inadvertently attended a Primrose League Ball. It was being held at the Grand Hotel, whither they had adjourned for supper, and the sound of the music, and the sight of women in evening dress, had so excited Mr. Thirkettle that the Professor paid for two tickets of admission. (There was some slight difficulty about getting Mr. Thirkettle in; but Professor Pounce unscrupulously presented him as the Oldest Primrose Leaguer in East Anglia, and promised that he should not dance.) They had eaten one supper already, but they ate the Primrose League supper as well, and the Professor bought a bottle of champagne. It was altogether the most glorious experience of Mr. Thirkettle's existence. For the last hour or so he was incapable of speech; but as they stood at length on the doorstep of his home, waiting for his daughter to come and let him in, he pulled himself together for a final effort.

"To-night," stated Mr. Thirkettle, "I seen life."

"I've enjoyed myself too," said the Professor courteously.

"I seen life!" repeated Mr. Thirkettle, swaying slightly on his feet. The door behind him opened, and he sat down. Over his head appeared the furious countenance of a middle-aged woman. Mr. Thirkettle ignored her: he was cataloguing his memories. "First there was that dam great cinema," he mused, "and then our fine conversation, and then a bellyful of richness 'mong females with their naked shoulders, and then there was driving in a motor car. There was—"

"Dad!" cried his daughter angrily. "Where ever you bin?"

"Seeing life," said Mr. Thirkettle. "Good night, bor."

"Good night," said the Professor. "Good night, madam."

Over the dissolute wreck of her parent Miss Thirkettle glared at him.

"If it's you led him into this," she said grimly, "you ought to feel shame. You might ha' killed him!"

As a matter of fact, though this was not known till next day, it seemed very likely that the Professor had.

CHAPTER 12

1

OLD Mr. Thirkettle lay moveless in a semi-coma, tightly clutching a champagne-cork. It was generally assumed that he was about to die, and that if he did Professor Pounce would have killed him. Many people thought that Sarah Thirkettle ought to get compensation; a smaller party thought the Professor ought to get a medal; the Professor's own dominant emotion may be gathered from a brief conversation he had with Nicholas on the Wednesday morning.

"Uncle Isaac!" called Nicholas, returning white-faced from his milk-round. He ran upstairs and knocked on his uncle's door. "Uncle Isaac! Something rather awful's happened!"

The Professor bounced out.

"To the Stone? You mean someone has—mutilated it?"

"No, sir. To old Mr. Thirkettle. They think he's dying."

Professor Pounce drew a long breath of relief.

"Thank heaven I was in time!" he ejaculated reverently. "I believe I have every word of our conversation fully noted."

Nicholas gripped the bannisters.

"I hope, sir, you'll be able to take as detached a view when you're had up for murder. I don't know what you did to the old man, but his daughter wants to have you arrested."

"Then you'd better type my notes this morning," said the Professor.

For one wild moment Nicholas had a vivid and thoroughly enjoyable vision of his uncle in the dock at the Old Bailey. It would serve him right. He did not actually wish his uncle to be hanged, but he felt that only the urgent possibility of such a fate could bring Professor Pounce to a proper sense of his own relative importance in a world population of two thousand odd millions.

2

The day wore on, overcast by rumour and apprehension. A panel doctor, hastily summoned, confirmed that old Mr. Thirkettle was indeed at death's door. The Thirkettle cottage was visited by a constant stream of potential mourners. To each Mr. Thirkettle dumbly displayed his cork: it was his prize, his trophy, the symbol of the life which he had so avidly seen, and which he seemed so likely to quit. It made a deep impression, for such a thing had never been seen, let alone handled, in Gillenham before; and there was a certain amount of rivalry as to who should be, in this respect, his legatee. He had nothing else to leave. His Old Age Pension had been regularly expended at The Grapes, his wardrobe was negligible; but a champagne-cork was worth having. "Will it to me," urged young Arthur, "and I'll keep it on my chimney-piece for all to see. I'll keep it in Grandad's ancient shaving-mug, so it'll be a memorial, like, to the pair o' you." Old Mr. Thirkettle blinked a horny eyelid and said nothing. He could not speak; but there was something in his attitude that suggested he was open to bids. "You will her to me, bor," said old Mr. Uffley, "and there'll be a fine wreath from Ipswich to rouse envy at your burying . . ."

The project of arresting Professor Pounce also occasioned a good deal of interest. He was directly responsible for Mr. Thirkettle's state, but Sarah Thirkettle, by laying too much emphasis on this point, rather alienated than acquired sympathy. As more and more details of the orgy came to light a feeling arose, particularly among the male part of the community, that for such a night out a man of Mr. Thirkettle's age might well be prepared to risk his life.

It was a pity, said old Mr. Fox frankly, that he couldn't have had a woman as well; but otherwise Professor Pounce's hospitality was awarded full marks; and in the bar of The Grapes, where all such questions were finally decided, it was agreed that the Professor need not be arrested until his guest was actually dead.

3

And now occurred a strange, a halcyon period, quite unlike any other part of the Pounces' stay in Gillenham. The village lay under the shadow of death, the Old Manor lay under the threat of a murder charge, and yet a curious happiness, a spell of moral and emotional fine weather, lightened the atmosphere. It was due to the presence of Bridget Crowner.

Her first visit was paid on that same Wednesday afternoon. She knew about Mr. Thirkettle, and with a delicate sympathy (in Nicholas' view misplaced) spoke only of the immense pleasure which Professor Pounce had so generously given. She charmed Mrs. Pounce effortlessly and completely: she went into Mrs. Leatherwright's kitchen, and Mrs. Leatherwright did not rebuke her. On Carmen, Bridget's effect was the most interesting of all: the former simply withdrew herself—not physically indeed, but, as it were, spiritually; she somehow managed to decrease the force of her personality. One could look at her without blinking. Bridget looked at her a great deal, in most frank admiration, and remarked to Nicholas that she would love to try to draw Miss Smith's portrait. "That would be half a crown an hour," replied Nicholas glumly; whereupon Bridget, learning of Miss Smith's fame, treated her with naïve deference. It was by far the best thing she could have done, for it precluded, in the most natural and even flattering manner, any approach to intimacy.

For the rest, her conversation showed her to be intelligent, but not particularly well-informed; she never said anything at all witty or unusual, but she was a very good listener. Her mind worked quickly and happily; when the Professor regaled her with a few of his choicer Norse legends, she at once planned simplified versions to pass on to her kindergarten, and made a note of the source-books. She evidently took her teaching very seriously, and also enjoyed it; she appreciated both its essential importance and the fun of its detail. She made the Professor a paper box and a paper bird, laughing at herself for her pride of craftsmanship; and then, from sheer force of habit (she said), made a box and a bird for Nicholas, so that there should be no unfairness. . . .

"One sees," observed the Professor, as Bridget was led upstairs by Mrs. Pounce to inspect family photographs, "how certain now hackneyed phrases must have arisen. 'A ray of sunshine,' for example; 'a sunbeam in the house.' To-day one can scarcely use them except in mockery; but how happy, how startlingly appropriate, they must once have sounded!"

Nicholas nodded. He was hoping, but faintly, that his mother had not brought with her her favourite photograph, of himself at the age of three.

"One can't protect them," said the Professor sadly.

"Protect whom, Uncle Isaac?"

"The young," replied Professor Pounce. "'The bloom of youth'—there's another phrase for you. Not the efflorescence, of course, but the fine delicate powdering of grace. It can't be preserved. It's got to go. But when one sees so many young people, as I do, in the process of losing it, it saddens one. One has to harden oneself. I dare say that's what's made me the tough old crab I am."

This softening of Professor Pounce was not the least remarkable manifestation of Miss Crowner's influence. It was very brief, however. The old man sat a moment longer in thought, then shook himself briskly and observed that there was no need for Nicholas to see Bridget back to the Vicarage, as he would do it himself. He did so at once, as soon as she came downstairs, leaving Nicholas and Carmen looking after them from the gate.

"Well?" said Nicholas, as they passed out of sight. "What do you think of her?"

Carmen gave him a long contemptuous look. Her personality had expanded to its full size again.

"You oughtn't to ask," she said. "You oughtn't to ask *me* about *her*. I know that if you don't. She's the sort that's too good for any man born, and she's too good for me to speak of. She's like—" Carmen paused, thinking. "Like Hail Mary, full of grace . . ."

Nicholas had never felt so justly rebuked in all his life.

4

"With a china dove upon her," bargained old Mr. Uffley. "Painted metal from Ipswich, with holes for sticking blossoms, and a china dove over all . . ."

He was referring to the wreath which should adorn, in certain circumstances, his friend's grave. Mr. Thirkettle said nothing. He had to be very careful. His ancient mechanism was still holding together, but only just. He silently refused all medicines (to which indeed the doctor did not press him) and was being fed on pap laced with brandy—the gift of Mrs. Jim. It seemed a miracle that he still breathed at all. Twice already his daughter, fearing the worst, had sent for Mr. Crowner; but each time, as the Vicar approached, the flutter of a sardonic eyelid at once relieved and disconcerted the mourners. Mr. Thirkettle still lived; and he still had his champagne-cork.

5

If the Professor was now cheerfully and frankly in love with Miss Crowner, Miss Crowner no less frankly proclaimed her affection for the Professor. They went for walks together, they went mushrooming, they played deck-tennis over the cord in the garden. Bridget played as well as Carmen, but she did not make the Professor look a fool. She beat him joyfully, and mourned aloud on the rare occasions when he beat her. They arranged a yearly meeting for every first week in August, and Professor Pounce invited her to every annual soirée of the Folklore Society of Great Britain and Northern Ireland.

Nicholas watched them with envy. Sometimes, observing the complete happiness of their relationship, he could almost have wished to exchange his own youth and vigour for his uncle's placid age. There was little happiness in love for him; all he knew was that here it was, it had come, and he would have to find some way of dealing with it. In a sense it was like discovering he had some ailment, a weak heart or hay-fever. Out of Bridget's presence he spent his time inventing long intimate conversations with her—dazzling in wit, touching in pathos—and opportunities to display heroism. He even found himself rescuing her from the banality of a fire. In her presence, he stood either dumbly grinning or gloomily a-stare. If in passing a tea-cup to her their hands touched, his hand tingled. As far as he could tell, her hand didn't notice. He carefully preserved his paper box and kept it in his breast pocket. He also became acutely conscious of the passage of time, and at any moment could have told exactly how many days and hours were left of her sojourn in Gillenham.

Most important of all, he no longer desired to kiss Carmen.

That hot uneasy passion was quenched; it took all his sophistication to convince himself that he was not ashamed of it. He wanted to confess and receive absolution. But confess to whom? To Bridget? To his uncle? To a boy's best friend, his mother? Nicholas recoiled from them all; but the need persisted; and finally, strangely, he confessed to Mrs. Jim.

He had not meant to, but he found her alone in the private bar just after opening time, and it was she who first mentioned Carmen's name, remarking that Miss Smith had been in the previous night.

"With Mr. Pye?" asked Nicholas anxiously.

"By herself. Paid for her own drink and went out again. She's a deep one, she is."

"She's very attractive," said Nicholas.

"She's all of that," agreed Mrs. Jim.

"In a certain way, of course," added Nicholas. "As a matter of fact, when we first came, I was a bit attracted by her myself."

"I don't blame you," said Mrs. Jim.

Nicholas stared into his glass.

"As a matter of fact, I suppose I was a bit of an ass about her . . ."

Mrs. Jim looked at him kindly.

"Like stealing jam, ain't it? You feel a bit sickish afterwards."

"That's it exactly. Especially . . ."

"Especially," finished Mrs. Jim, "when there's so many others have had their fingers in the same pot."

Nicholas felt slightly sick in truth.

"You don't know how you could have done it," he said, "afterwards, when you wish you hadn't."

"I shouldn't let it worry you," said Mrs. Jim. "I don't suppose it was more than kissing behind doors, and where there's a door handy and a piece like her behind, no young man's to be blamed. Jam's jam."

Nicholas grinned faintly.

"When is a door not a door? When it's a jamjar. . . ."

"That's better," said Mrs. Jim. "Now you forget all about it, bor, and have a drink on me."

They drank with great friendliness, and Nicholas made several other weak jokes, at all of which Mrs. Jim laughed appreciatively. She was debating in her mind whether it would be well to let young Mr. Pounce get tight and be sick in earnest; then she decided that he had been sufficiently purged already, and sent him off still rather voluble, but walking dead straight.

6

On his way back occurred two rather interesting episodes. In the first place, he met Carmen.

"Hello, stranger!" she said.

"Hello, jam-pot!" said Nicholas.

Carmen's eye hardened.

"You've been drinking," she stated.

"I have," agreed Nicholas, "but not much. Your hair's coming down behind."

He put his hand to the tawny knot. A week earlier the contact would have set every nerve quivering. An hour earlier he could not have brought himself to touch her. Now he bundled up the loose strands and tucked in the wisps without the slightest emotion. He was cured.

Carmen looked at him thoughtfully, and walked away.

7

Nicholas also walked on, in the opposite direction. He was feeling rather pleased with himself. But a minute later his new-found aplomb received a rude buffet. As though all his amorous past were bent on catching up with him at once, he was suddenly confronted by Mildred Hyatt.

It was really surprising that they had not met before, for if Nicholas, ever since the interrupted lecture on *Gone With the Wind*, had automatically gone out of his way to avoid Miss Hyatt, so had Miss Hyatt been going out of her way to avoid Nicholas. But so it was, and they now met for the first time—face to face at a rather awkward stile, without another soul in sight.

"Oh, hello," said Nicholas.

"Hello," said Miss Hyatt.

They were both appallingly embarrassed. In the mind of each all the circumstances of their last meeting were being accurately reproduced. Miss Hyatt was wearing the same orange polo-jersey, and Nicholas could not keep his eyes off it. With the common idea of getting away from each other as soon as possible they made a simultaneous attempt on the stile and found themselves practically cheek to cheek.

"Sorry," said Nicholas, backing down. "Let me help you."

"No, thanks," said Miss Hyatt.

She climbed over from her side and Nicholas climbed over from his. He felt he had to say something more, so he asked after her work. Miss Hyatt replied that it was going well.

"*Bluebell Court* okay?"

"Oh, quite," said Miss Hyatt. "By the way, though—I'm afraid I shan't be able to use your verses. They're just a little bit,"—she smiled brightly—"just a little bit too silly. Good-bye."

Nicholas arrived back at the Old Manor a completely sober young man.

8

"Doves be damned!" said Mr. Thirkettle.

They were the first articulate words he had spoken in days, and they were not at all what his attendants expected. Old Mr. Fox, old Mr. Uffley, young Arthur and the panel doctor, who all happened to be sitting round the death-bed, exchanged startled looks.

"He's wandering," said young Arthur.

"No, I b'aint," said Mr. Thirkettle—faint but firm. "I'm speaking to James Uffley there, who's bid me a fine metal garland from Ipswich with a china dove fixed a-top. . . ."

Mr. Uffley nodded eager agreement.

"And I say, Doves be damned," reiterated Mr. Thirkettle. "I'll take a couple o' pints, every day I ask for 'em, and James Uffley shall have my fine champagne-cork which I brought back from that dam great feast."

There was a brief silence, a silence filled on all sides by the most intense, the most frantic calculation. From the look of him it seemed certain that Mr. Thirkettle could not hold out another twenty-four hours, but he had already held out, contrary to all nature, for nearly a week. Mr. Uffley reached across and plucked the doctor by the sleeve.

"Come outside, bor," he muttered, "and give us the odds . . ."

Chapter 13

1

With the first reappearance of Mr. Thirkettle at The Grapes the strange idyllic interlude ended. He crawled out into the sunshine, heavily muffled in many an ancient shawl, more tortoise-like than ever, and triumphantly demanded his two pints. For the doctor had let Mr. Uffley down: he had given the odds against his patient's recovery at thirty to one, and Mr. Uffley had closed. The champagne-cork was in his possession, but now, as he watched his friend thoughtfully supping his beer, he was assailed by doubts. With every throatful Mr. Thirkettle seemed to gain strength; nor was his first toast in any way reassuring.

"Here's to my very good health!" said Mr. Thirkettle.

The company drank it. They could hardly do less, when he had so lately been given up for dead.

"Two pints whenever I ask for 'em," continued Mr. Thirkettle dreamily. He fixed Mr. Uffley with a fond yet malicious eye. "You thought I was gone, bor, and I don't blame you. But now I'm going to make the ancientest bones this parish has ever seen. And 'cause for why? 'Cause I now," said Mr. Thirkettle, with emphasis, "I now got something to live for."

2

The day of Mr. Thirkettle's revival was the day of Bridget's departure, and a day, therefore, of extreme agony to Nicholas Pounce. He spent the morning in unhappy wanderings, the afternoon as a wretched chaperon to the cheerfully affectionate farewells of Bridget and his uncle; but after tea he went out and posted himself blatantly at the Vicarage gate. He had come to a desperate resolution: he was going to propose.

It was the first time in his life he had even contemplated such a thing, and he was not very optimistic. Indeed, his only hope—and how slender a one!—lay in his complete ignorance of Bridget's sentiments towards himself. She had always treated him with great friendliness, but then she so treated every one; if she was concealing a responsive passion, she was doing it very cleverly. But then she would naturally take care not to reveal her own feelings until she was sure of his—a Victorian theory to which Nicholas now instinctively subscribed without even noticing that it was Victorian. Under its influence he had concocted one particularly cherished day-dream in which her answer to his declaration was simply, "Oh, Nicholas, at last!"—after which the clouds of glory so swamped him that he never got any further. He felt that to hear Bridget say "At last!" he would willingly give ten years of his life; only he did not know who would take them. . . . There ought, thought Nicholas wildly, to be some sort of superhuman Exchange and Mart in which such transactions could be arranged: a year of a young man's life for a kind word, five years for a kiss, ten—twenty, thirty!—years to hear Bridget say, "At last!"

The Vicarage door opened, and she came out. Nicholas clutched the gate-post. She was wearing a dark blue coat with a white collar, and shoes with high heels, evidently her town outfit, but her head was bare.

"Bridget!" called Nicholas huskily.

She looked towards him and smiled.

"What is it? Have I forgotten something at the Manor?"

Only my heart, thought Nicholas. It would have been a rather lovely and romantic thing to say, and strictly accurate as well, but he could not get it out. For a long time afterwards he wondered whether it would have made any difference.

"No," he said, "no, nothing. Bridget, come for a walk."

"How can I? I'm leaving in about ten minutes!"

"Just a short one," said Nicholas obstinately. "Just down the lane. Just for the last time."

He pushed open the gate and waited. He was directing upon her, though he did not know it, though he did not mean to, the dumb, relentless persuasion of the dog that must be taken for a walk or die. Bridget came slowly down the path, and out beside him.

"Just down the lane, then," she said. "Just for the last time."

The hedges on either side made a green and private tunnel. Two persons, so narrow it was, could not walk within it without their hands occasionally touching. Nicholas kept his eyes fixed on the path; the breath came short in his throat, there was a queer thickness in his ears, as though he were under water. He had to speak now, it was his last chance, but he was forced to moisten his lips twice before he could do so.

"Bridget—"

"Yes?"

He moistened his lips again.

"I suppose you wouldn't think of marrying me?"

He could not look at her, but he felt, at his side, her start of dismay. "Ten years!" prayed Nicholas desperately. "Twenty, thirty years!" But it was no use.

"Nicholas, dear—"

"It's all right," he said tonelessly. "You don't have to explain."

"But I want to . . .

"I didn't expect anything else, really. Only—only it seemed silly not to ask while I had the chance. It's all right."

They walked on a few paces in silence, and he felt her hand slip through his arm. Idiotic, thought Nicholas angrily, to refuse to marry a fellow, and then go and touch him. Not fair. Then he looked round at her, answering her pull, and all anger faded.

"I'm so sorry," said Bridget. "It's not—it isn't anything to do with *you*. But I shan't think of marrying any one for some time."

"I'll wait, if it's any use."

"I don't think it would be, Nicholas dear. You see, you're not old enough."

"I should be older after I'd waited."

"I mean old enough compared with me. I hope it's not bothering you."

"Well, I can't sleep," said Nicholas.

Bridget looked really distressed.

"Have you tried taking a glass of hot milk before you go to bed?"

Her voice was softened by genuine sympathy, Nicholas considered her lovely candid face, her sweet uncomprehending eyes, and suddenly turned to pluck at a leaf-spray in the hedge. It was no good trying to tell her. It would be like trying to pull open a bud before it was ready. She simply hadn't the first idea of what being in love was like.

"All right, I'll try milk," he said.

He wasn't angry with her. He felt suddenly and purely protective. He felt he wanted to give her advice.

"I suppose people fall in love with you all the time?"

Bridget considered this gravely.

"A good many do. Or they say so. It's sometimes rather bothering."

"I hope you're careful," said Nicholas anxiously.

"I don't mean men in trains," said Bridget.

No, thought Nicholas, looking at her, she wouldn't be bothered by the genus Man in Train. Unless, of course, he were drunk. . . . The reflection started a new line of thought.

"I hope you're careful passing pubs and places? I mean, if there's a bus stop outside a pub, and another a bit farther on, I think you ought always to wait at the other one."

She nodded seriously.

"I know. I do get spoken to sometimes, at night, but it's never more than 'Hello, Goldilocks,' or something silly like that. Mostly from workmen and messenger-boys and people. I think they'd be terribly surprised if I said anything back. Lately," added Bridget, wrinkling her brows, "they've taken to 'Hiya, Toots.' I think it's because of the American films."

Nicholas shuddered. The idea of Bridget thoughtfully registering the picking-up phrases of the metropolis sent him into a cold sweat.

"Promise me," he said earnestly, "you'll *never* say anything back!"

"I never do. But I'll promise if you like."

"And if any one really bothers you, tell 'em what you told me. Tell 'em to try hot milk. It had a very pacifying effect."

Bridget turned and looked at him squarely.

"You think I'm a perfect child, don't you? You think when you say 'love' I don't know what you're talking about?"

Nicholas was silent.

"I don't know," said Bridget. "That's true. But I can imagine."

No, you can't, thought Nicholas. Not the hot uneasy part, not the dreams and desires that won't let you sleep in your cool uncompanioned bed. You can't imagine that, my darling. . . .

"I'm not funking it," said Bridget. "I'm just waiting."

They had come back to the Vicarage gate. She stopped and put out her hand and let Nicholas hold it while he said how much he looked forward to seeing her again. There was nothing else to say. She wasn't waiting for him. Nicholas hoped she was waiting for some heroic doctor, some prince among artists—for some mere titled millionaire even, so that her photographs might adorn and purify the illustrated press. But he very much feared she was waiting for some poor-souled elderly rotter with a weak chest.

"Carmen was right," he muttered. "There isn't any one." And before Bridget could question him, turned and went away.

3

So the interlude ended. Bridget was gone.

Once again, age had the best of it. Nicholas walked on through the evening, revisiting every spot which had been hallowed by her presence, and from each hedgerow or meadow plucked a flower. They were mostly dandelions, all he could find. He wasn't behaving in the least like Nicky Pounce of John's, who liked his women mature. He was behaving like a lovesick calf, and didn't care. The Professor, on the other hand, retired to his study and at once forgot all about Miss Crowner in the interest of drafting an invitation to the ladies of Gillenham to come and have their chastity tested on Saturday midday.

He drafted it in the form of a public notice, as follows:

TRIAL OF CHASTITY

A Trial of Chastity will be held next Saturday, at twelve noon, at Bowen's brook. Will any lady wishing to enter kindly sign below. No entrance fee. It is emphasized that all who take part will be contributing to a valuable scientific experiment, & your co-operation is earnestly desired.

God Save The King.

(Signed) ISAAC POUNCE.

The Old Manor.

Then he went out to look for Nicholas, whom he met returning down Manor Lane carrying a small bouquet of wilting greenery.

"What's that for?" asked the Professor, momentarily distracted. "Salad?"

"No," said Nicholas.

"Dandelions make quite good eating," remarked the Professor informatively. "At any rate the leaves. With oil and vinegar, of course."

Nicholas thrust the shabby bunch into his pocket. He felt sore and ill-used. Bridget was gone, the light of his life with her, and he couldn't even bring home a pathetic little keepsake without his uncle wanting to eat it. . . .

"What you need," said the Professor sharply, "is occupation. Are you any good at lettering?"

"Fairly, sir. What sort?"

"Gothic," said the Professor, producing his draft. "I want this doing out, poster size, without delay." Nicholas took the paper. Up to that moment he had believed he could never again feel any emotion unconnected with Miss Crowner; now he discovered that where his uncle was concerned, he could still feel apprehension.

"What do you mean to do with it, sir?"

"Put it up, of course."

"In the village?"

"Naturally. On the church door."

"I shouldn't," said Nicholas.

"Why not?"

"Well, sir, the Vicar mightn't like it. I'm sure Mrs. Crowner won't. And the church is rather their pigeon."

"Absolute nonsense!" declared Professor Pounce. "Church doors, from time immemorial, have been the recognized notice-board of every rustic community. I shall certainly make use of them."

"All right," said Nicholas wearily, "I expect it'll soon come down."

"Not if you do it properly. I am as well aware as you what is due to Mr. Crowner's susceptibilities. That," explained the Professor complacently, "is why I said 'Gothic.' If you don't know what Gothic is, get your mother's prayer-book and find out."

4

That same evening the car that bore away Bridget crossed another and a larger car containing two persons who (as has been said before) have very little to do with this history. They were the Unionist agent, Mr. Pomfret, and James Coulter, M.P. For it was Wednesday night, the night of young Mr. Coulter's address on Decimal Coinage. Both the Spriggs had ratted, Lady Sprigg because she genuinely had influenza, Sir Peter because his wife's indisposition furnished so providential an excuse that he felt it would be unlucky to ignore it. So Mr. Coulter and Mr. Pomfret arrived in Gillenham alone.

"I'm afraid," said the latter, "I shan't be able to do more than introduce you, and then disappear. We've guests to dinner, and I promised Mrs. Pomfret I'd be back by seven sharp."

"Very good of you to turn out at all," said Mr. Coulter.

The agent did not contradict this. Members of Parliament had no glamour for him. He felt that this one in particular would have done far better to stay quietly at home until his Party summoned him out.

"You mayn't have much of an audience," he warned. "I shouldn't call Gillenham specially politically minded."

"I'm not talking to 'em about politics. I'm telling 'em—"

"Quite," said Mr. Pomfret. He had no desire to hear the speech before it was delivered. He hoped, with luck, not to hear it at all. "Here we are," he said. "We've got the room behind The Grapes—very respectable house indeed. I'll just have a word with Mrs. Jim before we go up."

Mr. Coulter, with some idea of not making his appearance too common, waited outside till the agent reappeared and bustled him in by a side door. They went up a flight of stairs, through a second door, and emerged upon a small platform at the end of a long narrow loft. Behind them was a sort of back-cloth painted with palms, red curtains, and a medallion portrait of Queen Victoria; before them a score of benches were occupied by about thirty persons, mostly men. At the sight of the agent they shuffled perfunctorily with their feet, at the sight of Mr. Coulter they merely stared. On the platform were two chairs, a bamboo table, and a pile of old hat-boxes which Mrs. Jim had forgotten to clear away.

It was not an exhilarating set-up, but Mr. Coulter, like the war-horse saying "Ha!", cleared his throat and beamed all round, with a special beam for Mr. Pomfret. They both sat down, and then Mr. Pomfret stood up again.

"Ladies and gentlemen," he said, "it gives me great pleasure to bring here this evening Mr. James Coulter, M.P., who will talk to you about Decimal Coinage. I won't take up any more of your time, as I know you are all anxious to hear him. Mr. James Coulter."

There was another perfunctory shuffle as Mr. Coulter rose and advanced. He was in full fig of white tie and tails, and now he wondered whether they were a mistake. Surveying those stolid bucolic rows he felt a little like his fellow countryman of legend who nightly donned a stiff shirt to eat grilled monkey in the jungle. But there was no time for such reflections; the feet were shuffling again.

"Good evening, all," said Mr. Coulter jovially. He was always jovial with rustic audiences. He would have liked to say "Good evening, folks," but felt it was too much of an Americanism. One had to be very careful.

"Good evening, all," said Mr. Coulter therefore. "You don't know who I am; I'm not your Member; your Member is Mr. Muirhead, whom you do know very well—"

"Never set eyes on 'im in me life," observed a voice conversationally.

Mr. Coulter looked towards the back rows and caught the small sceptical eye of the elder Fox. He decided to ignore it.

"—and who has kindly allowed me to come here," continued Mr. Coulter, "to tell you something about Decimal Coinage. I won't call it a subject very near your hearts, because I dare say you haven't so far given much thought to it; but after to-night I hope you will.

"Now I dare say you all, at school, went through the same trouble that I did with your four farthings to the penny, your twelve pence to the shilling, your twenty shillings to the pound. To say nothing of half-crowns and florins, and that little devil the threepenny-bit. It's a miracle we don't still have groats to deal with! But consider the American child, the French child. Do they have to wrestle with these peculiar fractions and sub-fractions? Not they. A hundred cents make a dollar, a hundred centimes make a franc. That's all. That's literally all they have to learn. You've learnt it now, in five seconds. And when we come to weights–does the American child, for instance, bother about the stone?"

For some reason the audience, hitherto sheeplike in its apathy, sat up. Mr. Coulter felt encouraged.

"Not he!" cried Mr. Coulter, more jovially than ever. "He calls it fourteen pounds, which it is. We, for some peculiar reason, persist in calling it a stone. What good that does us I don't know–"

From somewhere at the back came a second voice, this time feminine.

"What about the Stone o' Chastity?"

"I beg your pardon?" said Mr. Coulter.

"I said, What about the Stone o' Chastity?"

Mr. Coulter paused uncertainly.

"The stone of *what*?"

"Chastity!" bawled a dozen voices at once.

Mr. Coulter, now completely at a loss, looked round for his chairman. But Mr. Pomfret, true to his word, had quietly left the platform a few minutes earlier.

"My girl Vi'let," continued Mrs. Brain (for she it was), "says it's all the Government. And *I* say, What about it?"

"I'm afraid," said Mr. Coulter, "I haven't the least idea what you mean. . . ."

"Ain't you in Parliament?"

"Certainly I am."

"Then you ought to know what they're at. My girl Vi'let she says they're going to take it up–"

"Take what up?"

"Chastity!" bawled the chorus.

Mr. Coulter felt for a handkerchief and wiped his brow. The heat was really oppressive. There was no water on the bamboo table. . . .

"The Decimal System," he began again, "has at least one cardinal advantage: that of simplicity. And what greater merit—"

"Us ain't *asking* you 'bout simplicity," pointed out Mr. Fox patiently.

"What are you asking me, then?"

"We've told you, mister. About the Stone o' Chastity."

"*He* don't know nothing 'bout chastity," observed another voice wearily. "He's from London."

"My dear sir . . . !"

"Mah dah sah!" mimicked Tom Fletcher.

"—if you put any reasonable question—"

"*He* don't think chastity reasonable!" explained the weary one.

Mr. Coulter wiped his brow again. He felt he was going mad.

"I've come here," he shouted, "to talk to you about the Decimal System. If you don't want to hear me—"

"Us don't give a dam one way or t'other," remarked Mr. Fletcher frankly. "What us *do* want to know is—what about the Stone o' Chastity?"

The door leading off the platform was very handy. Mr. Pomfret had even left it ajar. James Coulter looked at it with longing. He had never before abandoned a meeting in mid-speech, not even when the eggs flew, but he had begun to think that his reason was even more important than his principles. He opened his mouth for one final effort, and at that moment the audience began to sing. Softly at first, then with increasing *brio*, the fine old tune of "John Brown's Body" gathered way. Only the words were not the right ones.

"Grandma's body lies a-mouldering in the grave,
Grandma's body lies a-mouldering in the grave,
GRANDMA'S body lies a-mouldering in the grave,
But her SOUL goes marching on!"

Before the force of that last bellow Mr. Coulter instinctively recoiled. He glanced over his shoulder, and met the painted, fish-like eye of Queen Victoria. By a trick of the pigment she, too, appeared to be regarding him inimically. "Come, come, Mr. Coulter!" she seemed to say. "Lord *Beaconsfield* would have known how to handle them!"

It was the last straw. He couldn't take a chastity-mad audience in front and Queen Victoria in the rear. With one ghastly backward smile, Mr. Coulter fled.

5

He had an awkward moment getting his chauffeur out of the bar; the man seemed surprised that the meeting was so soon over. So did Mrs. Jim. So did the rest of the company—one of whom courteously explained that he had not attended the meeting himself as he would be able to hear all about it from those who had. "My God!" thought Mr. Coulter. He would have liked a stiff whisky-and-soda, but there was no time; he was too anxious to get away before the room above emptied. The chauffeur knocked back his beer and reluctantly followed him out.

"Last meeting we went to," observed the chauffeur dispassionately, "wasn't over till closing time."

"Wasn't it?" said Mr. Coulter.

"Not it. But that was one of Mr. Muirhead's."

Mr. Coulter did not reply. He privately considered Muirhead a pompous old bore, but he naturally could not say so. He said nothing at all, all the way back. He just rested. He very much hoped that Sir Peter would have gone to bed; but even by the time they arrived home it was still very early.

"You're soon back," said Sir Peter. "Good meeting?"

"Excellent," said Mr. Coulter. "I kept it short, though. I don't believe in tiring one's audience."

He had decided to say nothing whatever about his fantastic experience. It was too extraordinary, too incomprehensible. There was also the danger that it might strike his host (a man of crude humour) as slightly funny.

"What sort of folk are they in Gillenham?" he asked.

"Oh, just the usual sons of the soil," said Sir Peter. "Nothing special about 'em."

Mr. Coulter decided that in future he would leave rural England strictly alone. It was altogether too much for him.

He went to bed a very puzzled young man. His subsequent career in Parliament was a useful and happy one, marred only by one idiosyncrasy. He would never have anything to do with Agriculture.

6

In the bar of The Grapes, Grandma Powley's body mouldered, her soul still marched. Jim and Mrs. Jim, taking the compliment to themselves, stood a free round. Old Mr. Fox piped high and clear, the organ-like chest-notes of young Arthur enriched the basses; Mrs. Jim let her voice rip in stunning coloratura. The melody soared, swelled, and rocked the roof. It was audible far down the street, and in the houses on either side, where women clearing up their kitchens heard it and began to hum. Soon all Gillenham was singing, the tide of harmony surged gloriously through its alleys and byways, lapping at door-sills, throwing its spray against the windows, falling back only before the two impregnable rocks, the Vicarage and Vander's Farm.

"Charles," said Mrs. Crowner, "can you hear singing?"

The Vicar nodded.

"A little merry-making at Mrs. Jim's, I imagine . . ."

He sighed; he had a sociable nature, but also a strong sense of what was due to his position as a clergyman of the Church of England.

"They're singing 'John Brown's Body,'" said Mrs. Crowner.

"And a fine song it is," said the Vicar. "If we had a few hymns with such a swing, such a rhythm—"

"But they don't sing the right words, Charles." Mrs. Crowner put down her inevitable mending and clasped her hands tightly in her lap. "I don't know how to express it, but it—it's something to do with that dreadful Mr. Pounce. Charles, when are you going to speak to him?"

"Never, it seems," said her husband regretfully. "You won't let me."

"You know what I mean. You're too easy-going, dearest. You allowed Bridget to spend half her time with that man—"

"It hasn't done her any harm."

*"Nothing could do Bridget harm," stated Mrs. Crowner proudly. "But—Charles, listen!"

A favouring gust of wind brought the melody suddenly closer, wafting through the open window the clear, the almost defiant affirmation of the immortality of Grandma Powley's soul.

"Doesn't it sound—somehow *active*, Charles? As though something were going to happen?"

"Let it," said the Vicar.

He was undoubtedly almost a saint; but there were times when his wife wanted to hit him.

7

"Hark!" said Mrs. Pye sharply.

Mr. Pye turned his head,

"George," he said, "back from The Grapes."

"He's singing—"

"Aye."

Mrs. Pye got up and opened the door, so that her long black shadow, magnified against the lamplight, fell monstrously across the yard.

The singing stopped.

8

Not a note, not a beat, reached as far as the Old Manor, for the wind was blowing the wrong way; but the soul of Professor Pounce, no less than the soul of Grandma Powley, was in marching trim. His brief holiday in the company of Miss Crowner had recharged an already adequate store of pugnacious energy: he thought of the coming Trial of Chastity, he thought of his nephew's weak-kneed objections, and he laughed aloud. His sister-in-law heard him, Nicholas heard him, and to both the sound was definitely ominous.

"Nicholas, dear," said Mrs. Pounce nervously, "do you know what your uncle is laughing at?"

"No," said Nicholas—not quite truthfully. "But I think he'd better laugh while he can . . ."

"What *do* you mean, darling?"

"I think he's for it," said Nicholas. "I think we're all for it. If I were you, Mother, I'd go straight back to Town."

Somewhere across the fields a cock crowed. From the Professor's room above came an answering crow of ancient mirth.

"Nicholas," said Mrs. Pounce, "darling, I'm so glad *you're* here!"

"I'm not," said Nicholas.

CHAPTER 14

1

THE next morning was one of intense activity. The Professor went out early and enlisted the services of young Arthur to help him replace the Stone in its original position. Nicholas, with a certain vindictive enthusiasm, set about the poster. He got red and black ink, and a large sheet of drawing-paper, and made the whole thing look as sacred as possible, framing the letterpress in thick black lines with crossed corners. He hoped the Crowners would scent blasphemy and take it out of his uncle. Professor Pounce, however, returning hot, happy, and rather wet about the trouser-cuffs, was quite struck.

"You see what you can do when you try," he said encouragingly. "Give me the drawing-pins, and I'll go and put it up before lunch."

Nicholas gave him the drawing-pins, smiling grimly as he did so. Then he saw the Professor off, and himself went upstairs to brood a bit over his dandelions. He had placed them, with tender care, between the leaves of the heaviest book he could find, and it happened to be a bound volume of the *Boy's Own Paper* for 1880, which he discovered in the bottom of his wardrobe. But as soon as the blossoms were properly pressed, he meant to transfer them to the more appropriate pages of Keats' *Endymion*.

2

By two o'clock that afternoon there were nineteen names on the Professor's list: those of Mrs. Jim, Mrs. Ada Thirkettle, Sally Thirkettle, Grace Uffley, Violet and Mabel Brain, Mrs. Jack Fletcher (all in the hand-writing of the first), and twelve Boy Scouts.

By three o'clock the poster had been torn down. There was no evidence as to who had done this, except that it was Mrs. Crowner's day for cleaning the church brasses. Fortunately the Professor had already visited the poster once and made a note of the first seven signatures. (The dozen Boy Scouts he rightly ignored.) He came back in high feather, and Nicholas later found him in his study drinking gin and French and ruling neat columns in a handy notebook. They were headed, according to plan, for Name and Age, Comment, Common Knowledge, Result, and Marking. Nicholas could not help feeling a certain interest; he looked at the list of names, and commented with surprise upon so large a number.

"And that's not all," said the Professor happily. "Not by any means."

"Who else have you got, sir?"

"Well, there's Carmen for one," said Professor Pounce.

"Carmen, sir? You mean *she's* going to try?"

"Of course. That's what she's here for. While scarcely hoping for such good fortune, I naturally did not come unprepared. I had to be certain of *one* subject."

Nicholas gaped.

"You mean she . . . ? I mean—Well, sir, in which sense?"

"If Carmen doesn't slip, the whole thing's discredited. And it's a very fair test—very fair indeed," said Professor Pounce, with growing enthusiasm, "because her physical reactions are excellent. She won't slip through nervousness, or lack of balance, or anything like that. Indeed, if the legend is correct, no virgin could slip, just as no loose woman could keep her footing; but I wished to make a perfectly fair trial."

Nicholas unobtrusively helped himself to a gin and French. He was speechless. The mystery of Carmen's presence was at last cleared up: she was nothing more nor less than a guinea-pig. It was astounding. It was also, when he thought of all the agony he had endured on her account, somehow vaguely insulting to himself. It was, he thought angrily, the limit. But he thought wrong. His uncle's limit had not yet been reached.

"Then there's your mother," continued the Professor brightly.

Nicholas pulled himself together.

"Have you spoken to her yet, sir?"

"No, I haven't; but, of course, she must assist. And—"

"Well, I don't think she'll care about it. I don't really, sir."

"Why on earth not?" demanded the Professor. *"She has nothing to fear. I witnessed her marriage myself."

"But she's not very steady on her feet," pointed out Nicholas uneasily. "You should see her on an escalator. And aren't you rather assuming, sir, that the Stone does work? Suppose it's just an ordinary one and Mother skids—"

"In that case Carmen will have kept her footing, and the whole thing is invalidated. It's simple."

"Then why can't you work it with Carmen alone? As you say, she's the perfect subject."

For the first time the Professor displayed a slight embarrassment.

"In a sense," he admitted, "that is true. Indeed, it's entirely true. I mustn't prevaricate. But in my monograph—well, a goodlier array would be more impressive."

Nicholas was touched. He had not suspected his uncle of so much human weakness. In his mind's eye he saw the old boy rising, paper in hand, to address a gathering of fellow folklorists. *We now come to a most interesting series of tests . . .*

"You won't put the actual names in?"

"Certainly not," said Professor Pounce—rather too hastily. "Just A, B and C. Or rather Alpha, Beta, Gamma. Your mother shall be Alpha."

"All right," said Nicholas. "You try her, and I'll back you up. She can always wear a pair of flat-heeled shoes."

The Professor quickly added his sister-in-law's name, courteously placing it at the head of the list. Then he paused to reflect.

"What about that young lady at Rose Cottage? Miss Hyatt, I believe?"

Nicholas did not quite know what about Miss Hyatt. His personal experiences had left him in considerable doubt. He was inclined to put her down as a borderline case; but he could hardly describe her so to his uncle. Chivalry forbade.

"She's very shy," he hedged. "I don't think she'd care for the—er—publicity."

"There won't be any publicity. To a fairly well-educated young woman such an experiment ought to be highly interesting. I'm assuming, of course, that she's a virgin?"

"I've never asked her," said Nicholas gloomily. "And I'm dam well not going to."

Professor Pounce nodded.

"I think you're right. The question would come much better from another woman. Your mother—"

This idea filled Nicholas with such horror that he had to have another gin and French. Such a question, from Mrs. Pounce, after the episode of the previous week, would be the last insult. It would lay him open to the worst suspicions. It was not to be thought of.

"Look here, sir," he said violently, "if you have Miss Hyatt questioned in such a way, by my mother or any one else—"

"Don't shout at me, sir!"

"I am not shouting, sir!" Aware that he was, Nicholas lowered his voice. "All I want to point out, Uncle Isaac, is that just because you happen to know a spot or two about Norsemen, you have no right to go about the country molesting respectable young women."

"God bless my soul!" said the Professor.

Nicholas himself felt that he had put the case a bit strongly.

"All I mean to say, sir—"

"You had better say nothing. To argue a point rationally is one thing, to back inept opinions by vulgar abuse is another."

"I'm sorry, Uncle Isaac."

In stern silence the Professor shuffled up his papers and rose.

"I shall go and look at those ferrets," he announced coldly. "Their company will be a refreshment and a relief."

"May I come with you, Uncle Isaac?"

"No, you may not," said the Professor, stalking past. At the door he turned. "A *spot* or two about Norsemen!" he repeated. "Good God!"

Chapter 15

1

One of the things that annoyed Nicholas most about his uncle was the latter's knack of drawing the right conclusion from the wrong premises, and thereafter taking credit to himself for his perspicacity. This trait was particularly noticeable in the case of Mildred Hyatt, who called the next morning for the express purpose of offering her services in the cause of folklore.

"My dear young lady," exclaimed Professor Pounce delightedly, "*I* was just about to call on *you* to make that very request. As I told my nephew here, when he seemed to think you might be unwilling—"

Miss Hyatt fixed Nicholas with a cold eye.

"Why was that?" she asked.

Nicholas shifted uncomfortably.

"I thought you'd be too busy . . ."

"That wasn't what you said before," observed Professor Pounce. "However, what *I* said was that a well-educated young woman like yourself might be relied upon to take a proper interest."

This was not quite true: "fairly well-educated" had been the Professor's phrase. Nicholas would have liked to catch his uncle's eye, but was too much afraid of catching Miss Hyatt's instead.

"Of course I'll help," said Mildred Hyatt. "I'd love to. I suppose all you want me to do, Professor, is to walk across the stepping-stones without falling in?"

The Professor nodded. In his heart of hearts he wished Miss Hyatt to keep her footing only if she deserved to and he could prove it. In his heart of hearts he would willingly have sacrificed her reputation to a really striking footnote in his monograph. But he could hardly say so.

"Of course, Miss Hyatt won't fall in," said Nicholas impatiently. "The whole thing's bunkum."

As he realized at once, it was not a tactful remark to make. Mildred Hyatt turned her back on him and began talking very rapidly and brightly to his uncle.

"You know, I'm not sure so," she said. "I don't believe in the supernatural part, of course, but I do think, psychologically, there may be something in it. As there was in so many of those old tests. I mean, suppose an unfortunate girl had a guilty conscience, mightn't that affect her motor reactions? On a slippery stone, with every one watching, mightn't she quite easily fall out of sheer nervousness? And there you'd have your magic proof."

The Professor beamed.

"My dear young lady, you have put my own theory better than I could myself. And I am sure it is the correct one."

"Then in that case," said Miss Hyatt deliberately, "the test is still working." She turned back to Nicholas. "Don't you agree, Mr. Pounce?"

"In a sense, I suppose it is," muttered Nicholas.

"So that I shall be very pleased indeed," finished Miss Hyatt, returning to the Professor, "to come and help. I mean, if it had been simply play-acting, I shouldn't feel any interest. If you want to use my name, you may."

"Thank you," said the Professor heartily, "I certainly shall."

"It's Mildred Mabel Hyatt, 17 Fraser Mansions, Bloomsbury. I'll write it down."

She pencilled it on a slip of paper. The Professor in his enthusiasm offered her a glass of sherry, but she refused. She also refused one of Nicholas' cigarettes. It was plain that she did not wish to stay in the same room with him a moment longer than was necessary, because he contaminated the air. But her parting from the Professor was most cordial, and he came back from seeing her to the gate still beaming with approval.

"What did I tell you?" he demanded.

"You told me she was fairly well-educated," replied Nicholas bitterly, "and you also expressed doubts as to whether she were a virgin."

"Well, I haven't any now," said the Professor.

"Nor have I," said Nicholas.

"I've always been a believer in female education," continued Professor Pounce complacently, "and what we have just seen is one of the happy results."

With a great effort, Nicholas said nothing.

"And you were wrong about your mother, too," added the Professor. "I've just spoken to her, and she is not only willing to assist, she is even anxious."

"That's surprising," said Nicholas.

"To you, perhaps. Not to me. The fact is," said Professor Pounce, "you don't know as much about women as I do—"

Nicholas could not remember ever having been so annoyed by his uncle before.

2

A good many other people were annoyed by Professor Pounce; the Professor didn't notice them either. He was too completely absorbed in his plans for the morrow and his dreams of his monograph. He was even capable of passing Mrs. Pye, as he did later that morning, and of raising his hat to her, without marking the fanatic gleam in her averted eyes. A few moments later he met Mrs. Crowner, and Mrs. Crowner cut him dead. The Professor raised his hat again and went innocently on. In his pocket was a fresh notice to replace that torn down from the church door; he meant this time to leave it at the Post Office. Nicholas would not have attempted such a thing, but the Professor blithely and blindly entered the shop, found it empty, and attached his notice to the grille marked "Stamps." He had no idea of avoiding trouble; he simply remembered that at that hour the Postmistress took her dinner, and refrained from disturbing her. On his way home he met the girl Sally, who at his friendly greeting nervously dropped her eyes and backed into the nearest door; Professor Pounce considered this a very pretty example of rustic simplicity. In Manor Lane he overtook a muck-cart conducted by one of the younger Fletchers; scarcely had he passed it when something caught him between the shoulders with a soft thwack. "What was that?" demanded the Professor, wheeling round. "A Cromwell's blessing!" shouted young Fletcher, with a grin. The Professor was enchanted. He looked down at the broken gobbet, and remembered how Hindus anointed their door-steps with urine for luck; while the resurgence of the Great Protector's name in familiar speech provided food for delightful thought all the way home. Professor Pounce returned to the Old Manor as happy, and as ignorant, as he had left.

3

Before the door stood a small disreputable two-seater. The Professor looked at it carefully, noted an easel projecting from the dicky, and deduced that it belonged to a friend of Carmen's, and that the friend was a prominent rebel rather than a successful R.A. Both these deductions were a moment later confirmed by the appearance of Carmen herself and a tall middle-aged man with paint stains on his cuffs. Immediately after them came Nicholas carrying two bottles of beer.

"Hello," said Carmen. "This is Mr. Alexander. Shall you want me this afternoon?"

"No," said the Professor, "and I hope Mr. Alexander will lunch with us."

"Had it, thanks," said the artist.

"Carmen hasn't," put in Nicholas pointedly.

"Sandwiches in the car," said Mr. Alexander. "Light's just right. Ready?"

He took the beer bottles out of Nicholas' hands, stowed them carefully in the hood, with less care helped Carmen into the car, and drove off. He was evidently as single-minded a man as the Professor himself.

"He's been here exactly ten minutes," observed Nicholas, as they disappeared. "I call it dam rude."

"Why?" asked Professor Pounce.

"He turns up here, bones two bottles of beer, carries off Carmen—"

"She asked my permission."

"—and hasn't time for common civility."

"You feel neglected," remarked the Professor. "But Mr. Alexander had something to do. I imagine he wishes to make a drawing of Carmen."

"And the light was just right!"

"And the light was just right," agreed Professor Pounce seriously. "When that happens, one daren't waste time. When the light is right for one's work everything else has to go. You don't know that yet, of course."

"Why of course?" asked Nicholas jealously.

"Because you've never done any work. I'm not saying it's entirely your fault; you have no strong natural bent."

Nicholas sat down on the high door-step. Though the conversation was not very flattering he wished it to continue, because it was about himself. He had long felt that his uncle did not take enough interest in him.

"I can write quite decent light verse," he offered.

"Psha!" said Professor Pounce.

In a flash of honesty Nicholas realized that the observation was just. He had felt no real compulsion to write those verses about Bluebell Court. He had written them partly to get money, partly as a first step in the seduction of Mildred Hyatt—and then he hadn't even seduced her. . . .

"You're a dilettante," said the Professor, unconsciously meeting this thought. "When I remember your father—"

"That's probably why," rejoined Nicholas glumly. "It's reaction."

Professor Pounce cocked his head.

"An interesting modern trend," he murmured. "Instead of visiting the sins of the fathers on the children, one visits the sins of the children on the fathers. Because my brother Ephraim happened to be an exceptionally upright and hard-working man, you, his son, consider yourself entitled to loaf through life like a lizard with lock-jaw. Why don't you find something to do?"

"It's not so easy," muttered Nicholas.

"Have you offered your services to your father's Bank?"

"Good God, no!"

"Did your tutor make no suggestion when you went down?"

Nicholas did not immediately answer. His tutor, a man in some ways rather like Professor Pounce, had prefaced an unemotional farewell with the single comment that a term in one of His Majesty's prisons might possibly help Nicholas to acquire the habit of regular work.

"He made no suggestion at all, sir."

"Then I will," said the Professor briskly. "It's just occurred to me. I happen to know that Professor Mostyn requires a tutor for his three sons. Their ages range from five to eight, so you should have little difficulty in keeping one step ahead of them; and I will write to-night recommending you for the post."

"But—good Heavens, sir—!"

The Professor waved all protests aside.

"I haven't much regard for the fellow," he explained. "An inaccurate scholar, a loathsome stylist, and a vegetarian. You'll do for Mostyn, all right."

"But really, Uncle Isaac—"

"Don't argue," said the Professor. "I've had you on my mind long enough. You can go on writing light verse in your spare time; for example, after you have put the boys to bed."

Nicholas swallowed.

"Does he want a tutor, sir, or a nursemaid?"

"He wants both," explained the Professor frankly. "Using 'want,' that is, in its common connotation of 'need.' But he can afford only one. Quite rightly, he puts education first. When you write to him yourself—"

"I have no intention of writing to him," said Nicholas coldly.

"Perhaps you're wise. Your hand might discourage him. Leave it all to me."

"Look here, Uncle Isaac—"

"Now let's have lunch," said Professor Pounce.

4

It was an unsatisfactory meal, partly because the chicken ordered in the village had failed to arrive, partly because the Professor lost no time in informing his sister-in-law that the question of Nicholas' future was now decided. "It may not be brilliant," admitted the Professor, "but it will be a career of quiet usefulness . . ."

Mrs. Pounce looked at her son with tender eyes.

"I'm sure that's just what Nicholas wants," she said. "Isn't it, darling?"

Nicholas looked back at her and wondered how the hell, after knowing him for twenty-two years, she had the nerve to make such a statement. He almost preferred his uncle's bullying, which was at least realistic. But he knew he could not argue with his mother without raising, so to speak, his father's ghost: an immaculate phantom pointing sternly towards the brat-ridden domicile of the vegetarian Mostyn.

"I've had enough," said Nicholas, pushing back his chair. "If you'll excuse me, Mother, I think I'll go for a long walk."

"Don't tire yourself, dear," said Mrs. Pounce fondly.

"If you see any of our friends from the village," called the Professor, "you might remind them of tomorrow's treat."

5

The luncheon, or rather the dinner-table, at Vander's Farm was very different from that spread at the Old Manor. There were a couple of ducks, one hot and one cold, and a great round of spiced beef, and potatoes and cabbage and cheese and pickles and an apple pie. On this fare Mr. Pye stoked himself methodically for half an hour without haste, but also without speech. Opposite him his wife displayed an equal appetite. Food was her only sensual indulgence; yet her body, as though in disapproval, refused to put on an ounce of flesh.

"Pye," she said, when the meal was over, "what are the men at to-morrow?"

"Carting," replied Mr. Pye briefly.

"Happen I'll want a couple round noon."

"The want must be your master," said Mr. Pye.

"I tell you I must have them."

"And I tell you they're carting."

"And I say carting can wait."

Mr. Pye stared at her suspiciously. His wife interfered daily with his comfort, his religion and his morals; she had never before interfered with his farm.

"You'll be learning me my trade, now?"

"This is none of your trade—unless you make it so."

"What d'you want my men for?"

"I want 'em to do my bidding."

"They'll do mine," said Mr. Pye.

He stood up. His wife stood also. Her dark, almost fleshless face was set like a mask. She said:

"I want George and Tom for to be at Bowen's with me. If I can't have 'em, it'll be the worse for your new whore."

This was the first overt reference she had ever made to Carmen Smith; but he did not pretend to misunderstand her.

"Worse nor a ducking?" he asked grimly.

"It's not her I'd ask 'em to lay hands on. I wouldn't ask a decent man to touch her. It's the old 'un. Him that started it all."

"Then you're a greater dam fool than I thought you. Mr. Pounce is gentry."

"Water'll wet him just the same."

"And he'll bring an action against two of my men—with harvest in sight. Why can't you let it alone?"

Mrs. Pye's voice suddenly rose.

"Because I'm a Christian woman and it's my place to wrestle with the ungodly! Because I can't stand by and see wickedness done without lifting my hand against it! Because the Lord's laid His task on me, and I can't shuffle it off!"

"He's not laid His task on my men," said Mr. Pye. "You leave Parson's work to Parson, and let me to mine."

He walked heavily out. For some minutes his wife stood rigid with anger; then automatically she laid her hand to the dishes and began to clear the table. Her thoughts moved slowly in the deep rut worn by days of bitter plotting, to be brought up again and again by the obstacle of her husband's stubbornness. Stubborn and stiff-necked he was, like all men born: his mind set on worldly goods, heedless of moth and rust. He was consumed by them already—the rust of evil thoughts, the moths of lust: the great silken moths whose soft bodies she crushed each evening as they flew to her lamp.

Mrs. Pye jerked her thoughts back. She knew from experience that if she let her mind dwell on wickedness she sometimes lost as much as an hour from her day. And there were no hours to lose; the night was coming when no man could work—no woman; what did men know of the Lord's work? It was the women who did it all, the righteous women, yoked to unbelievers, yet striving against evil nevertheless . . .

It was the women who must do that work now. Mrs. Pye left the still-littered table and went to a small back room where her toady Mrs. Fletcher sat mending sheets.

"Sarah," she said, "put that by and come with me." Mrs. Fletcher gave her one look, then laid the linen aside.

"Is the time come?" she asked.

"Aye. Though not as planned, for we must do alone."

"It's in your mind still?"

"It's in my mind to put an end to this heathen wickedness that's stalking abroad through Gillenham. It's in my mind to terrify that evil man from his morrow's sinful doings."

"We'll be going to Old Manor, then?"

"Not yet," said Mrs. Pye grimly. "We go first to the village. To rouse the women . . ."

CHAPTER 16

1

TO HAVE his future settled, in five minutes, casually, upon a door-step, is enough to make any young man angry; when the young man happens to be any one so distinguished as a Nicky Pounce of John's, it makes him very angry indeed. Nicholas tramped on through the lanes, injured and furious. His uncle had simply popped him—or thought he had—into the nearest vacant pigeon-hole, just as though he, Nicholas, were no more than a mere common encumbering out-of-work. As though his requirements were no more than food and lodging, and money to buy cigarettes. As though his special omni-potentialities could find adequate stimulus in a household of three brats and a second-rate dominie . . .

"Insufferable!" thought Nicholas Pounce.

He did not know quite what he expected his uncle to do about him—except that it ought to take longer. He did not know quite what he expected the world to do about him. Sometimes he felt that its function was to remain passive—his oyster, in fact; sometimes he felt it ought to bestir itself. The world at large, as opposed to the world of Cambridge, had so far taken no notice of him at all: no literary editor, remarking those really rather exceptional verses in the *Granta*, had summoned Nicholas to join his staff: no distinguished Parliamentary guest at the Union debates had offered him a private secretaryship. Like a great many other young men who had gone down at the same time, Nicholas, while not actually expecting either of these things to happen, kept the possibilities at the back of his mind, where they did a fair amount of harm. They had made it, for instance, quite impossible for Nicholas to consider following the paternal footsteps into the National and Shires Bank; they now made the descent to a tutorship even more abysmal. They made the whole outlook of Professor Pounce slightly ridiculous and entirely invalid.

The question that remained was, what was Nicholas to do instead?

He decided, most regrettably, to begin by borrowing a hundred pounds from his mother, and taking rooms in Town, and mixing with useful people.

It was his impression that useful people were most likely to be met at the Savoy.

It is quite sad to have to record such things of Nicholas, but he even reflected that many useful people had daughters. (Where now was the lovely image of Bridget Crowner?) He cold-bloodedly considered vamping the daughter of any useful person, his intentions, of course, being strictly and cynically honourable. (Poor Miss Hyatt, where was she?) He did not even trouble to visualize his future wife: she could look, for all he cared, like the back of a cab. (Alluring, exciting figure of Carmen Smith, Minoan barmaid, where are you now?)

As a matter of fact, the figure of Carmen Smith was at that moment surprisingly visible. Nicholas had reached a gate on the edge of the Pye property, and he could not but see over it into the pasture beyond. It was a charming pasture, smooth and green, adorned by a single tree; and under the tree stood Carmen stark naked.

2

For an incredible moment Nicholas did not recognize her. With her clothes had gone her vulgarity: she was noble. She stood perfectly still, her head a little turned, one arm raised, the hand resting on a bough whose shadow threw a mask over the upper part of her face. For one moment

Nicholas stared at her as impersonally as at a cloudy sky or a branch in the wind; then he saw that it was Carmen; and still he could look unmoved except by impersonal beauty.

A male voice spoke.

"Rest," said Mr. Alexander.

Carmen dropped her hand, stretched, and stooped to pick up something at her feet. It was her tweed coat; she slipped it on, belted it, and at once her bare legs and throat became disreputable. With no other thought than the averting of a scandal Nicholas leaped over the gate.

"Carmen!" he shouted. "Get indoors!"

She turned and stared at him. The artist turned also, eyebrows raised.

"I assure you—" he began.

"I know," said Nicholas, feeling slightly ashamed of his heat. "It's perfectly all right as far as I'm concerned. Only here—if any one were to pass—it might be a bit awkward."

The artist shrugged.

"Awkwardness," he said, "is a thing I'm used to. It's not important. What is important is that line of shadow crossing the line of shoulder."

"To you," agreed Nicholas. "And to me," he added, remembering his reputation as an aesthete. "But Carmen—"

Carmen left no doubt as to what was important to her.

"It's five shillings an hour, for outdoors," she said simply.

Nicholas swore under his breath.

"I'll pay you seven-and-six for the rest of the time."

But Carmen shook her head. As always when money was concerned, her peculiar streak of honesty asserted itself.

"I've been paid," she said, "for two hours, and there's still half to go." She turned to the artist. "You want me to go on, don't you?"

"If you're rested," said Mr. Alexander absently. "You can have five minutes more."

For answer Carmen stood up and unbelted her coat. At that moment Nicholas heard voices in the lane behind him: he turned and saw bobbing above the hedge two female hats. They were both of black felt, skewered by hat-pins—unmistakably hats of the village—and they were a few yards from the gate.

"Carmen!" shouted Nicholas.

It was the worst thing he could have done. It drew attention. The hats paused and pressed closer to the hedge, then bobbed on again at an accelerated pace. Carmen, defiant and uncomprehending, thrust her coat from her shoulders and moved back to her place under the tree. She reached it just as Mrs. Pye and Mrs. Fletcher reached the gate, and so turned her body to their full view.

Mrs. Pye screamed.

The sound was dreadful in its hatred. Surprise and anger were there also, but it was the hatred that made Nicholas sick. He looked at the black lean figure pressed against the gate and saw it was indecent, because it made indecency where none had been. He was also afraid, because he had not seen hatred before, and his youth was appalled by it. Instinctively he ran towards Carmen, shielding her body with his own as he would have shielded it from a bullet; but the artist was there before him, holding Carmen's coat to her arms. He too had seen, and his face, as he spoke over his shoulder, was twisted as though at some bitter taste.

"That's finished it," he said. "I'm sorry, young 'un. Shall I try to explain to them, or leave it?"

"Leave it," said Nicholas huskily.

"Then take Carmen to the car while I collect my traps,"

Still keeping between her and the gate, Nicholas shepherded Carmen across the pasture. Of the three of them she was much the least moved, her attitude being still purely professional.

"I never will have people looking on," said Carmen crossly. "Memorizing, like as not. Why should they, when they haven't paid?"

Nicholas felt pretty sure that there had been memorizing on the part of Mrs. Pye. He wished that his own memory of the whole incident were not so clear. He made no comment, however, nor did the artist as he drove them back to the Old Manor. But he glanced several times at Nicholas' troubled face, and before leaving them at the door suddenly pulled out his sketch book and ripped off a leaf.

"Keep that, young 'un," he said. "And remember that's the truth of it."

Nicholas looked, and saw a rough sketch of Carmen's raised arms and head and noble breasts. Beauty that endureth forever. . . . He went into the house still troubled, but assuaged.

3

He spent the rest of the day in a state of extreme uneasiness, which was not allayed by a brief conversation, about five o'clock, with Mrs. Jim. He met her in one of the lanes, so far out of her usual orbit that he felt certain their encounter was no accident, and after the first polite greetings there fell a constrained silence.

"Look here," said Nicholas at last, "have you heard anything in the village about—about this afternoon?"

Mrs. Jim nodded her blond, profusely-hatted head. There was a lot in hats, thought Nicholas suddenly: Mrs. Jim's was no dusty black felt, but a blue rose-crowned straw. It was a generous hat, an expansive hat, a hat one could trust. . . .

"We've all of us heard," said Mrs. Jim regretfully.

"What?"

"Don't ask me, for I won't tell you. That woman's got a mind like a muck-heap with her tongue for rake. But it was—it *was* a naked woman and two men, bor?"

Nicholas winced.

"In a sense it was. But—"

"No need to explain to me. I've lived in London, I have, I know them painter-fellows' ways. Often there's no harm in the world where there looks the most. I believe you, bor. But for the rest of 'em it's just Sodom and Gomorrah naked and unashamed. In fact," finished Mrs. Jim, with no sense of anticlimax, "there's a lot of feeling—"

"I was afraid there would be," said Nicholas.

"Bad feeling," said Mrs. Jim. "Mrs. Pye, she's been going from door to door, and what's in her mind I couldn't say, for she kept clear of me all right. But from door to door she's been going, and she's traipsed now 'way over to Old Farm. In fact, if you'll pardon me speaking, and you know I'm never a one to meddle, I'd say Mr. Pounce ought to give up his to-morrow's pranks."

"He won't," said Nicholas unhappily. "You don't know him."

Mrs. Jim shook her head till the roses in her hat incongruously danced.

"Are you going to let him down, too?" asked Nicholas.

"A publican's like a parson," said Mrs. Jim gravely. "They got to keep in with every one. And the same for me, like it's the same for Mrs. Crowner. I'm sorry, bor. If it wasn't for my Jim I'd stand by Mr. Pounce against the lot of them.

But my Jim—" She broke off, evidently remembering something unpleasant.

"He said to tell you," she went on slowly, "if you was thinking of looking in at The Grapes to-night—"

"I wasn't," said Nicholas quickly.

"Then that's all right. We do hate trouble, Jim and me."

She shook her head again, but this time almost absent-mindedly. She was looking about her as they walked, and Nicholas saw that she had imperceptibly guided their steps to the scene of the afternoon's encounter.

"Is this the place?" asked Mrs. Jim.

Nicholas nodded. She stared over the gate with frank curiosity, evidently checking up on previous information. Then she shook her head for the third time.

"It's just as I made out, bor. Who'd choose a place like this for their games? There's not cover for a rabbit!"

"Did you say that to Mrs. Pye?" asked Nicholas eagerly.

"Not I. I didn't get the chance, nor I wouldn't if I had. When you come to my age, there's thoughts you keep to yourself. There's thoughts you keep *from* yourself, 'cause your youth's over and naught'll bring it back. Not but what," added Mrs. Jim philosophically, "a bed takes a lot of beating."

She took a last look before turning away: at the green, springing grass, at the bright straight tree, the pattern of shadow on trunk and ground.

"It must ha' been a pretty sight," said she.

4

But if from Mrs. Jim, as from the artist, Nicholas received a certain comfort, he still felt that they were mental allies rather than physical: they had helped him to throw off the memory of Mrs. Pye, but they still left him holding, so to speak, the baby who was his Uncle Isaac. A heated argument after dinner left the Professor unmoved: the morrow's ceremony should go forward in spite of all opposition. Not that the Professor expected opposition; he did not exactly laugh his nephew's fears to scorn, he simply ignored them. He could not get it out of his head that the village of Gillenham would be rather delighted than not with the whole proceedings. Even the defection of Mrs. Jim could not shake him; he said she would come along fast enough when she saw all the others. "But there won't be any others," argued Nicholas despairingly. "If Mrs. Jim won't come, none of them will."

"Nonsense!" retorted the Professor. Nicholas had never in his life come across such an awful example of wishful thinking.

Immediately after dinner he went out and wandered about the fields until weariness drove him to sit down on a stile in Manor Lane. He was too restless to go back to the house, and too apprehensive. He was not quite certain what he feared: trouble, in Mrs. Jim's vague phrase, was undoubtedly brewing; but in what shape? What had Mrs. Pye been up to? Had he presented himself that night in the bar of The Grapes he would quite probably have been thrown out; the notion of tar and feathers recurred to his mind. If the Professor persisted in what Mrs. Jim—again so vaguely—termed his "to-morrow's pranks," would the tar and feathers be made over to him? Nicholas had a brief vision of his uncle black and beplumed; that would be bad enough, if the old boy tamely submitted. But the old boy would not tamely submit. Not he. He hadn't enough sense. . . .

From these unhappy meditations Nicholas was suddenly aroused by the sound of feet. The sound of many feet, not exactly marching, but proceeding in unison. He stood up on the stile and from that elevation was able to see over the hedges round the next bend of the lane. It was full of women. To Nicholas' startled eye there seemed to be an army of them: in the van strode Mrs. Pye, the rearguard was lost in the gathering dark, and here and there above the obscure mass rose the sharper outline of weapons. They were only umbrellas, but Nicholas received an impression of pitchforks. For a moment he stood agape and motionless; then a sudden realization smote him from his perch. The line of that fearsome cohort's advance led directly, and only, to the Old Manor.

Nicholas took to his heels and ran.

Chapter 17

1

"Uncle Isaac!" panted Nicholas, bursting through the Manor door. "Where is he?"

Mrs. Pounce, halfway down the staircase, looked at her son with gentle surprise.

"In his room, dear. He's just going to bed. I do wish you wouldn't be so noisy."

Nicholas leapt up and past her. On the landing he turned. "Bolt the front door!" he cried. "Bolt all the doors! And the windows!"—and dashed along the corridor to his uncle's room. The Professor, already in pyjamas, was brushing his teeth.

"Uncle Isaac!" cried Nicholas. "They're coming!"

With maddening deliberation the Professor rinsed out his mouth.

"Uncle Isaac, they're *coming*!" repeated Nicholas desperately. "They're almost here!"

"Who are?" enquired the Professor.

"The women! Mrs. Pye, sir, and dozens more! I've just seen them in the lane—"

"They probably want your mother," said the Professor calmly. "It's late for calling—"

"They aren't calling, sir. And they don't want Mother. They want you!"

"Now, let's get to the bottom of this," began the Professor, setting his tooth-glass down on the windowsill. "You say you've seen Mrs. Pye, whom I take to be the wife of Mr. Pye at Vander's Farm—"

Nicholas strode across the room and seized his uncle by the shoulders. He almost shook him.

"You don't understand, sir—you never *would* understand—the feeling this investigation of yours has aroused. Half the women are furious about it. They feel insulted. And they're out for your blood. Now. They've got pitchforks—"

At that moment, like the first ominous roll of thunder, sounded the first knocking at the door. Professor Pounce cocked an ear.

"There they are," finished Nicholas, in grim triumph. "They're here."

The knocking, now augmented by the percussive power of three umbrellas, was renewed.

"They do sound," admitted the Professor, "a little impatient. Is the door—"

"Barred," said Nicholas. "But they can easily break a window. You must hide at once."

Professor Pounce uttered a snort of derision.

"Hide! From a pack of women!"

"You haven't seen them, sir. I have. They look like—like the French Revolution."

"Then according to all the films," said Professor Pounce cheerfully, "the correct procedure is to meet them at the head of the stairs. You, Nicholas, will stand on my right, your mother will cower to the left—"

"Uncle Isaac!" cried Nicholas wildly. "This is serious!"

"So were the films," retorted the Professor, "or meant to be. Where's your mother? She must be coached."

At that moment Mrs. Pounce appeared. Like her son, she was in no mood for fun and games.

"Isaac," she said nervously, "there are dozens of women outside. They're shouting through the letterbox. What had I better do?"

"What are they saying?" asked the Professor.

"I can't quite make out. They're all shouting together. But there's something about a *ducking* . . ."

"I'll come down and speak to them," said Professor Pounce briskly.

Nicholas and his mother at once placed themselves before the door.

"I shouldn't, really, dear," said Mrs. Pounce. "They seem quite put out about something."

"Then I'll take Carmen as a bodyguard. She's as stout as any of them."

Between Nicholas and his mother passed an apprehensive glance.

"I shouldn't, really, dear," said Mrs. Pounce again. "I don't think they're very *fond* of Carmen. As a matter of fact, she did shout something from her window, and some one threw a stone up."

"Now *that*," said the Professor grimly, "settles it. Get out of my way!"

He advanced towards the door, he thrust his sister-in-law to one side; in another moment he would have marched forth to face the mob. But the mob was no longer before him, it was in his rear. An ominous sound from the garden below made Nicholas jump to the window.

"They're coming round!" he cried. "Uncle Isaac, get out!"

"Rats!" ejaculated the Professor.

With an air of clearing the decks he thrust Mrs. Pounce out and locked the door, and marched back to his nephew's side.

2

The scene upon which the pair of them looked out was not unremarkable. Still under the leadership of Mrs. Pye the women had effected a double Banking movement, and were now streaming round the house from both sides. Their black silhouettes—for all were clad in the sombre hue of their respectability—moved witch-like in the darkness: a couple of Mrs. Leatherwright's cats, strolling in and out on their nightly prowl, completed the effect. It was a Nonconformist Witches' Sabbath.

"God bless my soul!" exclaimed the Professor traditionally. Either his voice, or the lighted window, at once drew attention. Over the now serried ranks passed a quickening stir; and out to the front stepped the gauntest, most witch like figure of them all.

"There he is, the Villain!" cried Mrs. Pye.

"That's you, Uncle," said Nicholas.

The Professor appeared surprised; and indeed, as he stood there in his blue-and-white pyjamas, his hair neatly brushed for the night, his teeth freshly cleaned, it would have taken a more than ordinarily suspicious eye to detect in him the appearance of villainy. But such was the eye of Mrs. Pye, such were the eyes of her henchwomen.

"Forgive my costume," said the Professor pleasantly. "Ladies, what can I do for you?"

"You can get out," replied Mrs. Pye distinctly. "You can stop your heathen wickedness and get out before you make this place a byword and a hissing in the mouths of the ungodly."

She brandished her umbrella at him. It was the long, old-fashioned kind, and reached very nearly to the window-sill. Several other women brandished their umbrellas also. But the Professor did not flinch.

"If you are referring to my research into your local legend," he said, "I can assure you that you are all under a misapprehension. The Stone of Chastity—"

"It's a heathen image!" called Mrs. Pye.

"It is not," retorted Professor Pounce, with some annoyance. "It is not an image at all. The testing of chastity—"

"An' who asked you," cried a shrill voice from the rear, "to come here testing of our chastity? That's what *I* want to know!"

It was what they all wanted to know. From the increasing hubbub of threats, imprecations and personalities, that one question emerged. As Nicholas had feared, the women of Gillenham were not in the least scientifically-minded. Ignoring all considerations of motive, they called the Professor in so many words a dirty old man. They surged closer beneath the window; the hindmost rank, having passed under the apple-tree, were armed with more than hard words. A first volley of unripe apples bracketed the window; the second volley scored two bulls, both on the person of Professor Pounce. Nicholas tried to pull his uncle back, but the Professor would not be pulled. He held on to the window-sill and shouted in ancient Greek.

The strange sounds had effect. To many of his assailants it doubtless seemed that he had suddenly gone mad. In any case, there was an immediate hush.

"I am now going to address this meeting," shouted Professor Pounce. "There are six apples inside this room, and in case of interruption my nephew here, who bowls for the M.C.C., will not hesitate to return them." He paused invitingly; no interruption came. "Right," said the Professor in more normal tones. "The meeting is now open. Ladies—Madam. Chairwoman and ladies—"

"He's calling us madwomen!" cried a voice.

The Professor leaned courteously out.

"Mrs. Pye at least," he said, "will exonerate me from that suspicion. As President of the Women's Institute she will recognize an accepted form of address."

Now this was a very crafty move. It at once placed himself and Mrs. Pye, if not in alliance, at least on the same plane of superior education. The lady turned and cast a repressive glance in the direction of the voice, and Professor Pounce seized the moment to get his oar in again.

"Ladies!" he said loudly. "I ask only three minutes. If at the end of that time your attitude towards me remains unchanged, I promise to come down among you and pursue the argument at closer quarters. But for the moment, from this more elevated position, I have a better chance of making myself heard."

He paused. Silence, not complete, but broken only by the shifting of feet, gave consent. Nicholas had an uneasy recollection of a story about a lion-tamer; lions were not dangerous, said the author, so long as they roared; but beware of the lion which stopped roaring to think. . . .

The Professor cleared his throat.

"I came to Gillenham, as you know, to pursue a piece of scientific investigation. In so doing I have had the misfortune to arouse the antagonism of the most intelligent section of the community—to wit, yourselves. The fault is entirely mine. Instead of demanding your collaboration, instead of going straight to the Women's Institute and seeking out its President, Mrs. Pye, I contented myself with—the word may seem ungrateful, but there is no other—I contented myself with riff-raff."

Ungrateful or not, the word went down very well indeed. To hear Mrs. Jim referred to as riff-raff undoubtedly filled many a long-felt want. From the listening ranks rose a faint grim murmur of satisfaction.

"With rag-tag," elaborated the Professor thoughtfully, "and bob-tail."

The murmur increased. Old in the arts of lectureship, Professor Pounce raised his tooth-glass and took a sip of its highly antiseptic contents.

"And why," he demanded rhetorically, "did I so content myself with riff-raff, with rag-tag, and with bob-tail? Because, ladies, I did not feel justified in pressing my own slight affairs on the more worthy members of the community. You are all busy women: excellent housekeepers, careful mothers, devoted to good works; you have—or so I assumed—no time for trifles. But my assumption was wrong; it is the busy woman who can find time for everything. If I had gone straight to Mrs. Pye, in ten minutes she would have set me right. She would have informed me, courteously but definitely, that the whole matter was repugnant to your natural delicacy—"

"I should so!" cried Mrs. Pye.

The Professor beamed at her.

"Thank you," he said. "I know you would. You would have spared me ten minutes of your valuable time, and saved me weeks of useless labour. I regret it all the more as I hear that you manufacture a most excellent ginger wine."

"None of it for you!" retorted Mrs. Pye.

"That is what I regret," said the Professor. "It took first prize, I believe, at the Ipswich show?"

There was a moment's silent struggle; then a natural pride won.

"Five year running," said Mrs. Pye.

"My daughter's took second!" cried a voice near the summer-house. "She'll give you a sup, mister, and welcome! She's not afeared of any one tasting *her* brewings!"

"Thank you," said the Professor warmly. "Mrs. Fox, is it not? And your daughter is Mrs. Alfred Uffley? I shall certainly call round at the first opportunity. Now, where are we?"

There seemed to be some doubt. A second voice from the rear volunteered the fact that her old man knew how to brew mead. A small group (centring round the summer-house) seemed to be of the opinion that Mrs. Pye had taken first prize not five years running, but four. "Divide and rule!" murmured Professor Pounce cheerfully; and the same thought, perhaps differently couched, must have entered Mrs. Pye's head also. She turned her back on the window and imperiously faced her troops.

"Now then!" cried Mrs. Pye. "Stop gabbling! We're not come here to maunder about ginger wine!"

"Oh, ain't we?" countered Mrs. Fox.

"Who," shouted Mrs. Fletcher, mistakenly loyal, "near killed Sarah Thirkettle's Dad? He did!"

"Aye!" cried Miss Thirkettle. "He did so!"

"Pity he didn't finish it off!" retorted Mrs. Uffley. "The old beggar's out now all right, taking two pint off my old man regular!"

"Given the old fool a new lease of life," added Mrs. Fox. "Sarah did ought to be proper grateful."

Mrs. Pye hammered with her umbrella against the brickwork.

"I'll tell you what we're come here for!" she shouted. "We're come to stop this wicked rogue making a heathen show of the whole village! Were here to stop his concubine roaming naked through our decent fields! We're here to tell him that if he carries on with his sinful work it's him that's going to be ducked in Bowen's! His three minutes is up long since, and has he said one word of we're right and he's wrong? Not him. He's just soft-sawdered you about your ginger wines, and you poor gabies," finished Mrs. Pye contemptuously, "know no better than to lap it up."

She ceased. Her oratory was almost as good as the Professor's; but she made two cardinal mistakes: that of showing her contempt for her audience, and that of reintroducing an irrelevancy.

"My daughter—" began Mrs. Fox deliberately.

"In thirty-five," stated a second voice, "'twas Mrs. Bassett. I remember clear as anything—"

The Professor seized his chance.

"All comparisons," he proclaimed smoothly, "are invidious. *Fiat justitia, ruat coelum*—" (Nicholas, who had hitherto felt that his uncle was using too academic a language, suddenly realized his error. It was a language associated in the mind of the Women's Institute solely with sermons, and the Latin tag completed the pulpit effect.) At once all heads turned back towards the window.

"Thus to enter any contest, to submit oneself to any trial," continued the Professor, "implies a certain degree of either moral or physical courage. Sometimes it implies both, as in the trial which I propose to conduct to-morrow. That, ladies, is why I refuse to be turned aside. I have spoken of riff-raff, of rag-tag: but in this riff-raff, this rag-tag, I have found the physical bravery necessary to cross a swift-running brook upon slippery stones, and the moral bravery that fears not to face a challenge to woman's dearest treasure. There is a certain natural sting about receiving a second prize for ginger wine: which of you would risk receiving a second prize for chastity? The ladies who assist me to-morrow take that risk because to their minds the risk does not exist: they arc secure in the consciousness of their own virtue: and I will not insult them by now withdrawing the opportunity of proving it."

The hush deepened. Then a low murmur, like the first hum of a disturbed beehive, rose from the whole garden. The Professor leaned nonchalantly against the window frame and looked out upon his work, and Nicholas looked at his uncle. His opinion of the old boy was undergoing a complete revision.

"Mister!"

The voice was tentative, but excited. Professor Pounce leaned out and peered through the darkness. A slighter, a more youthful figure had pushed forward from the ranks. It was the girl Sally.

"Mister Pounce!" said Sally. "*I'm* not afeared!"

Mrs. Pye laughed derisively. Sally spun round on her.

"I'm not!" she cried. "I know what you all think–"

"What we all know," corrected Mrs. Pye. "You and that young Cockbrow–"

"It's not true!" cried Sally. "It's a dirty lie!–And that's why I'll be tried like Mister Pounce wants, just to prove it! *I'm* not afeared!"

"Nor me neither!" cried Mrs. Fox. "Nor my daughter!"

The cry was taken up by more voices than one. It appeared that none of them was afraid. Mrs. Pye had to raise her voice to its loudest to dominate the tumult.

"Fools!" she shouted. "Letting yourselves be bamboozled by an old sinner! Him that lets his concubine go naked—"

"He won't want us naked!" cried Sally.

"Certainly not," said the Professor. "In fact, I should prefer all candidates to wear their Sunday attire. Such as have no Sunday clothes—"

"*I* got Sunday clothes!" called Mrs. Fletcher—ratting at last.

They all had Sunday clothes. A desire to display them in competition filled every breast. It was the Professor's most cunning stroke yet.

"Ladies," he said, "I will not press you. I will only say how delighted, how grateful I should be for your assistance to-morrow. I do not *ask* you to come—indeed, if any one of you feels the slightest nervousness, I would much rather she stayed away—but I may add that after our purely formal little ceremony there will be coffee and cakes here at the Manor. Arising out of which, my sister-in-law, Mrs. Pounce, bids me tell you that though all will be very welcome, she would be glad of a rough idea of what number to expect. A show of hands, please."

Every hand save one shot up. Only the hand of Mrs. Pye remained clenched at her side.

"Thank you," said the Professor. "I make it thirty-nine. There is only one more point: I learn that Miss Smith, the young lady who has come from London to assist me, has been grossly insulted by one of your number. Who it was cast that stone—who cast that first stone—I do not know. But there must be an apology."

Nicholas held his breath. There was one thing even his uncle could not do, and that was make any one of the village women apologize in person to Carmen Smith. But the Professor paused only an instant.

"I take it, then, that such an apology may be conveyed to Miss Smith by myself without delay. Thank you," said Professor Pounce rapidly. "Carried unanimously; the meeting is adjourned; good night."

CHAPTER 18

1

THE fateful morning dawned misty, with a promise of heat. By ten o'clock the mist had melted into thin streamers. By noon the sky was a clear and cloudless dome of blue. It was a perfect day for testing chastity.

The water of Bowen's brook, unruffled by the least breath of wind, slid tranquilly by. Not even the line of stepping-stones disturbed its flow: the gentle element parted and slipped between with scarcely a ripple. Nothing could have been more reassuring. The faces of the stones themselves were smooth and dry; only upon the Stone of Chastity, polished by long domestic use in the Thirkettle scullery, lapped now and again a small wet tongue. The space between stone and stone varied from two to three feet. The depth of water between them was nowhere greater than fourteen inches. On either side the bank sloped at an angle not more than one in twenty-five. (These figures, taken from Professor Pounce's note-book, lend point to Miss Hyatt's theory that the test was almost purely a psychological one.) Under the shadow of the new bridge, about twenty yards upstream, dozed a great pike—but not for long.

2

"It's a pity," said Nicholas thoughtfully, "we haven't a film unit here."

It was a pity indeed. Apart from the human interest, the assembly offered material for a sound documentary short on "Women's Dress since 1860." Mrs. Thirkettle wore a Paisley shawl bought at the Great Exhibition, Mrs. Uffley the bugle-trimmed jacket in which her mother had been married; the gap between such historic landmarks and the mass-produced art silks of the younger generation was bridged by many a strange bodice, bonnet and furbelow. An interesting figure was Miss Hyatt, who with a nice sense of the picturesque had put on a fresh print dress, white stockings and black shoes. (Nicholas very much wanted to know whether she was also wearing green garters, but their relations being what they were, he could think of no means of finding out.) Every woman in the village was present—except Mrs. Pye, who was at home with the blinds down, and Mrs. Crowner, who had carried the Vicar off to Ipswich for the day—and every man who could get away from his work. The Boy Scouts had turned out in full force, hopefully bringing their stretcher with them. In the centre of the throng stood Professor Pounce, holding his note-book and an indelible pencil; a little apart Nicholas chaperoned his mother and Carmen Smith. He had instructions to keep the latter as much as possible in the background; fortunately the task was made easy for him by Carmen's financial conscientiousness. She had her mind on her job, and cast not a single glance in the direction of the men.

"Now then!" called Professor Pounce. "To begin with, we'll have all the men on the opposite bank."

Tom Uffley shouldered forward with a grin.

"What, is us to be tried too, mister?"

"No," retorted Professor Pounce. "You go over by the bridge."

There was a burst of shrill derisive mirth as the men stumped reluctantly up the bank and straggled across. Their movement, and the laughter, broke up and animated the crowd. Professor Pounce ran up and down the female ranks entering names in his notebook. A Stop-Me-and-Buy-One ice-cream vendor, pedalling idly by, was galvanized by the size of the throng into furious salesmanship. "Name please!" urged the Professor. "Cornets, a penny and tuppence!" cried the ice-cream man. "Watch your step, old woman!" bawled the men crossing the bridge. "I've my eye on ye!"—and many a similar pleasantry. It was a most animated scene.

"Feeling quite happy, Mother?" asked Nicholas anxiously.

Mrs. Pounce nodded. She too was wearing her Sunday dress, a very nice spotted foulard, and her best walking shoes. She had absolutely turned down her son's suggestion of rubber soles.

"If you don't want to do it, Uncle's got dozens here without you."

"I do want to do it," said Mrs. Pounce. "I must do it."

"All right," said Nicholas. "Just take it easily, and don't get your feet wet."

It was a silly thing to say, as he afterwards realized. His mother gave him a curious look and turned to Professor Pounce.

"Don't you think it's time we began, Isaac?"

"Yes, I do," agreed the Professor, "Has any one a hand-rattle?"

No one had. He looked round, made a bee-line for the ice-cream waggon, and loudly sounded its bell. To Nicholas this was the most pleasing incongruity of all: a Trial of Chastity on old Norse lines opened by the bell on a Stop-Me-and-Buy-One. Or was there after all a curious, an uncanny appropriateness? The Norsemen had discovered America, and the Americans had discovered ice cream, and to both races the virtue of their women had always been a point of great importance. . . . But he had no time to follow up this fascinating line of thought. In the sudden hush his uncle spoke again.

"Now then," said the Professor, opening his book, "who will be Number One?"

"I will!" called Mrs. Jim.

She stepped proudly forward and let them all take a good look at her. She was magnificent. She wore a dress of flowered silk, loudly coloured in red, white and blue, and over it a light blue coat and a feather-boa. On her head was a brand-new hat, trimmed with upstanding bows. On her hands were yellow gloves. And on her feet were a pair of evening shoes with the highest heels ever seen in Gillenham.

"My dear lady," beamed the Professor, "I do not know which to compliment you on first—your appearance or your spirit. Allow me!"

Ceremoniously he conducted her to the brook's edge. The assembly pressed close behind. Mrs. Jim set her right foot on the first stone, her left on the second, her right again on the Stone of Chastity, and so marched triumphantly across into the arms of Jim on the farther bank. There she swung round, and with her hand in her husband's turned a beaming face upon the applauding crowd.

"How's that, you bastards?" called Mrs. Jim.

It was enough to start a positive stampede. The Professor, hastily noting Mrs. Jim as 100 per cent chaste, planted himself on the water's brink and heroically fended off the mob. "One at a time, ladies!" he cried. "One at a time, please! You will all have ample opportunity!" But still they pressed forward; the girl Sally dodged under his arm, gained the first stone, and ran successfully across. Half a dozen of the younger and more agile followed her; Professor Pounce clutched his book and desperately tried to take notes while the men on the bridge shouted encouragement. "Us'll keep score for you, mister!" they called. "Grace's over! Vi'let's over! Mabel's done it!" The Professor's pencil could not keep pace with them, the situation was rapidly getting beyond his control; he glanced round and caught sight of his sister-in-law.

"Mrs. Pounce!" shouted the Professor. "Next candidate, Mrs. Pounce!"

It was a wise move. The person of Mrs. Pounce commanded respect. She wasn't jostled. As she moved forward the women stopped pushing and left her a clear path.

"Thank you, Maud," said the Professor gratefully.

Mrs. Pounce did not look at him. She was staring at the line of stepping-stones. Nicholas followed her to the verge and saw her foot planted firmly on the first stone. She drew her other foot alongside it, and paused; from the older women rose a murmur of approval. *That* was the way to cross, slowly, with dignity, not leaping like a nanny-goat; Mrs. Pounce was a lady, she knew how; and the lead, specially to those who suffered from rheumatism, was very welcome. In this way Mrs. Pounce safely transferred herself from the first stone to the second, from the second to the third, and thus reached the Stone of Chastity.

She reached it, and she stuck.

"I can't!" wailed Mrs. Pounce.

The murmurs of approval changed to cries of encouragement. Mrs. Pounce was adjured not to look down, not to look up, not to look over her shoulder. Nicholas leapt forward, instinctively proclaiming that his mother had always been terrified of running water. From the other side Mrs. Jim shouted to her to make a dash for it. But Mrs.

Pounce stayed where she was, her small plump feet close together, her hands clutching at her knees, her face crumpled with dismay.

"It's all right, Mother!" called Nicholas. "I'll get you!"

He was already on the first stone, his hand out-stretched. But he was too late. At the sound of his voice his mother had looked round, half turned, and lost her balance. Before the eyes of all Gillenham—splash went Mrs. Pounce!

3

Half a dozen willing hands—those of Jim, Mrs. Jim and Nicholas himself—hauled her out. She was wet only as far as her waist, and only behind, for she had landed squarely on her seat; but a cry of brandy and blankets was at once raised from both shores. The Boy Scouts hopefully unfurled their stretcher, to be waved back by Professor Pounce, Mrs. Pounce could still walk; tenderly but rather urgently supported by Nicholas, she passed out of the throng.

"Next!" called the Professor.

Nicholas, one arm about his mother, managed to squint down at the note-book. Against the name of his sister-in-law the Professor had placed a large nought.

He was a very single-minded man.

4

There was no party at the Old Manor that day. With true delicacy the guests kept away, feeling no doubt that they could not flaunt their superior marks for chastity before a hostess who had received nought. Mrs. Leatherwright carried the trays of buns, the jugs of coffee, down to the field beyond the orchard, and there dispensed an alfresco luncheon. Rather to Nicholas' surprise, the Professor went out too; from an upper window-seat Nicholas discerned him apparently making speeches, giving toasts, and in general being the life of the party. It seemed a heartless proceeding, with his sister-in-law's underwear still steaming before the kitchen fire; but popularity had evidently gone to the Professor's head.

Nicholas came down from his perch and went slowly towards his mother's room. He had not seen Mrs. Pounce since she retired to dry herself, and had scarcely exchanged a word with her on their dripping progress back to the house. He was not anxious to do so now, but he knew she would be needing sympathy. She would probably also like a cup of tea; and Nicholas, partly out of pure kindheartedness, partly to put off the evil hour, turned at the head of the stairs and went down to the kitchen with the idea of making her one.

The kitchen was not, however, empty. Mrs. Leatherwright, bearing a pile of plates, had just come in by the garden door.

"Oh, hallo," said Nicholas. He did not know much about Mrs. Leatherwright, but had always obediently kept out of her kitchen and thus earned her remote approval. But he suddenly did not want to ask for a cup of tea for Mrs. Pounce. He did not want to mention his mother at all. On the other hand, he badly wanted to know how the rest of the candidates, and Carmen in particular, had fared.

"Hallo," said Nicholas. "All over?"

"Mr. Pounce is still speechifying," reported Mrs. Leatherwright dispassionately. "I'd say he's set for some time."

"How did it all go off after—after I left?"

"Most surprising well," said Mrs. Leatherwright.

Nicholas thought this over.

"All safe across?"

A rare smile lighted Mrs. Leatherwright's countenance.

"All," she said, "all of 'em, except Carmen Smith."

Nicholas whistled.

"*She* went a proper purler," added Mrs. Leatherwright with enthusiasm. "Strolled up brazen as brass, she did, with her chin stuck out like the Queen of Egypt" (Nicholas could see her; Carmen high-headed in the sunlight.) "Make way for Her Royal Highness, it was—and we made way quick enough; who wanted to rub shoulders with the likes of her?" (Nicholas could see it: the goggling jealous lines of women, the men gaping on the bridge.) "She started out as though 'twas nothing—one, two, and then 'twas the Stone. She must have set her foot sideways on the edge, not even looking where she went; for there she slipped, and there was a great splash, and there lay Her Mightiness in the water!"

"Was she hurt?" asked Nicholas anxiously.

"Not her. She picked herself up, brazen as ever. Right up the brook she walked, shin-deep, and under the bridge with the men upon it; and they looked down at her, and she turned her face up to them, with such a look on it they didn't say a word. And then she came out at the shallows beyond and stalked off across Vander's fields."

Like a Swan Princess, thought Nicholas, like a water-woman, like a creature of another element. What had the men on the bridge seen when they looked down into those extraordinary eyes? The reflection of their own male desires, but so naked, so unadulterated by convention and accepted morality, that their own eyes fell abashed? They had seen at any rate enough to silence them.

"I wish I'd been there," said Nicholas. His old feeling was flooding back. If he had been there, Carmen would not have had to make that defiant gesture alone. He would have gone to her, protected her, forced the respect she had had to enforce for herself. . . .

"It was a rare strange sight," agreed Mrs. Leatherwright. "I'll not forget it to my dying day."

The door opened and Carmen came in.

5

She was still damp; her clothes, partly rough-dried by the sun, clung exactly to her body. Mrs. Leatherwright gave her one look, and walked out.

On the table was a loaf of bread and some cheese. Carmen cut herself a good wedge of each and prepared to go out again.

"Carmen!" said Nicholas.

She paused. One hand was on the door, the other conveyed bread and cheese to her mouth.

"I can't talk now, I want to get into dry clothes."

"I don't want you to talk. I just want to tell you—"

"Tell me upstairs," said Carmen, opening the door.

Nicholas followed her. It was very difficult to speak beautifully and poetically, as he desired, to a person who persisted in eating bread and cheese while running upstairs two steps ahead of one.

"Carmen," panted Nicholas, on the landing, "I want to tell you how sorry I am I wasn't there when you—when you—"

"When I fell in," supplied Carmen. "It was all right."

"You must have been marvellous," said Nicholas. "Wonderful. But then you are wonderful. It must have been ghastly, after that fall—"

"That's all right," said Carmen again. "Don't you worry. I'm paid."

She went on up to her own room. Nicholas sat down on the top step and rested his head on his knees. Carmen's last words had simply thrown him all out again. He hoped she had not said anything of the kind to Professor Pounce. Nicholas had never been quite sure how much faith his uncle put in the power of the Stone, but he certainly set great store by his monograph; a doubt cast on Carmen's good faith would entirely spoil the evidence. Or had Mrs. Pounce done that already?

The thought recalled Nicholas to his original design. But he felt hot and hungry. He decided that he would first have a wash and get something to eat. One needed, after all, to be feeling pretty strong before offering consolation to a mother who had just got Nought for chastity. He rose and went along the corridor towards the bathroom. But as he passed Mrs. Pounce's door her voice sounded from within.

"Is that you, Nicholas?"

"Yes, Mother," said Nicholas.

"Come in, dear," called Mrs. Pounce. "I want to speak to you."

CHAPTER 19

1

MRS. Pounce was packing. She had nearly finished. As her son entered she turned, sat down upon a bulging suitcase, and looked him desperately in the eye.

"I'm going," said Mrs. Pounce. "To-morrow."

She was much calmer than Nicholas had expected. But he had never known her to pack so quickly.

"If you feel you must, darling—"

"Of course I must. I can never set foot in the village—outside this house—again."

"But Mother, every one realizes it was an accident—"

"It wasn't an accident," said Mrs. Pounce.

Nicholas stared.

"It's true," said Mrs. Pounce. Her composure was rapidly deserting her. She took out a handkerchief and screwed it nervously between her fingers. Her small feet, now in bedroom slippers, fidgeted and shifted on the floor. "It's true!" said Mrs. Pounce.

"What's true, darling?"

"About the Stone. As soon as I touched it I felt a—a sort of power that wouldn't let me move. And when I tried to, you know what happened. It's all true—and, oh, Nicholas! Your mother's not an honest woman!"

Greatly disturbed by this hysteria, Nicholas advanced and sat down beside her on the case and put his arms round her shoulders.

"Listen, darling," he said anxiously, "you've had a beastly shock—"

"Nothing to the shock you're going to get," said Mrs. Pounce, with unexpected grimness.

She drew away so that she could turn and face him, and for the first time since he could remember Nicholas waited with real eagerness to hear what his mother was going to say next.

"Your father, Nicholas—"

"I know," put in Nicholas automatically. "He was the best man—"

"He was nothing of the kind!" said Mrs. Pounce.

Nicholas simply couldn't believe his ears.

"If you say that again," went on Mrs. Pounce, "I shall scream. It's what you've been saying, you and your uncle, every time I've tried to tell you. I couldn't destroy your faith in him. I couldn't speak to any one, get the least sympathy or understanding. Now I've borne it long enough and you've got to know too. Nicholas, your father was not what he seemed."

"By Gum!" said Nicholas, He felt a sudden surge of interest, of hope, of affection. "What did he do?"

"He deceived me . . ."

"But how?"

"I was never," said Mrs. Pounce, "really married to him at all."

Nicholas nearly fell off the suitcase.

"The Stone knew," said Mrs. Pounce.

2

Her story was so simple, so human a tale of fecklessness, that it at once commanded belief. In 1909, when the late Ephraim Pounce was twenty-four, he was sent by his Bank to their Manchester branch, and in that town became enamoured of a beautiful barmaid. With a recklessness more surprising on her part than on his, they were secretly wedded; secretly, because the Bank did not approve the marriage of junior clerks. Miss Lovell retained her maiden name and profession, young Pounce continued to lead an outwardly celibate life. No offspring blessed the union. At the end of a year young Pounce was transferred to Bristol, and was forced to leave his wife behind. Miss Lovell some time later obtained a superior position in Sheffield. She at least was not a practised writer, the Manchester hotel tired of forwarding Ephraim's letters, and the correspondence at last entirely dropped. Both parties were rising in the world: Miss Lovell, flourishing behind a succession of ever more gorgeous bars, had no desire to dwindle into a housewife; to Ephraim Pounce, taking his work ever more seriously, the whole episode of his married life must have seemed like an astonishing dream. In 1914 the War further cut him off from his old life; a year later he quietly committed bigamy by marrying the future mother of Nicholas; from which point until his death in 1930 his life was a model of rectitude, self-sacrifice, and all the civic virtues.

Miss Lovell, however, remained officially Miss Lovell. Perhaps her first experience of matrimony had given her a mistrust of the estate, perhaps she was more scrupulous than her husband; her many attractions brought her a corresponding number of honourable suitors, but she said No to all of them. And then in 1938 there appeared on the scene the barmaid's ideal—a gentleman owning his own house at Brighton. Miss Lovell was now forty-eight, a magnificent figure of a woman with many years of autumnal bloom ahead of her; but at an age of serious consideration of the future. Miss Lovell considered very seriously indeed; and as a result of her meditations put a personal advertisement in every British paper requesting news of Mr. Ephraim Pounce.

The Professor, who read nothing irrelevant to his work, never saw it. Mrs. Pounce, who read the personal column of the *Telegraph* every morning, did. With a pleasant feeling of secrecy and importance she said nothing to her son, nothing to her brother-in-law, but wrote to the Box Number given. She expected a small legacy: what she got was a visit from the first and only Mrs. Pounce.

Mrs. Pounce, née Lovell, brought her marriage-lines with her; but she was in no sense a blackmailer. She dropped a courteous tear, but was obviously delighted to be assured of her husband's certified decease, and went back to Brighton promising never to breathe a word of the dead and buried past. In many ways she was an extremely amiable woman. But she left the current Mrs. Pounce in a state bordering on frenzy.

3

"I feel," sobbed Mrs. Pounce, as the tale ended, "as though I'd never really *known* him . . ."

"So do I," said Nicholas. "By Gum!"

He felt an overwhelming sensation of release. The knowledge that his immaculate parent had once slipped up—had more than slipped up, had committed a major crime—was like the lifting of a huge burden. He wished he had known sooner, while the old chap was still alive. He felt he could have been so much more respectful to his father had he known he was a bigamist.

"What was she like?" he asked curiously.

"Rather like Carmen," said Mrs. Pounce. "What Carmen's going to be like. Oh, Nicholas, how *could* he?"

Nicholas knew damn well how he could. He seemed also to hear a warning, yet an understanding, voice from the grave.

"I told myself," continued Mrs. Pounce, "I told myself again and again that it wasn't true. That it couldn't be true. I told myself that in spite of everything there was some mistake. Another man with the same names . . . But to-day, on that Stone, I knew."

Nicholas patted her gently on the back.

"After all," he consoled, "no one else knows. No one ever will. It's all over. I don't really see what you're bothering about."

"My poor boy!" said Mrs. Pounce.

"I'm not upset, honestly, darling—"

His mother looked at him.

"You don't realize what it means, Nicholas. What it means to *you*. My poor boy, you weren't—you weren't born in wedlock!"

This was indeed a new light on the subject. Nicholas considered it a moment, and found that it meant nothing to him at all. If anything, he felt that not being born in wedlock leant him a touch of glamour, of romance, that had previously been lacking. He felt suddenly much more ambitious, much more enterprising. But it was too soon to present this point of view to Mrs. Pounce.

"My dear mother," he said, "whatever may have happened in 1909, or in 1915, I still stick to my opinion: Father was the finest man who ever lived."

4

It was some time later, when Mrs. Pounce had recovered a moderate tranquillity, that the question arose as to whether or not the story of Ephraim Pounce should be made known to his brother. There was no doubt that the Professor would be delighted to hear it; it was testimony of the strongest, the most convincing sort. In fact, it was just what the Professor wanted, and Nicholas was all for letting him have it. But Mrs. Pounce was firm.

"He wouldn't listen to me," she said, "when I wanted to tell him, and now he shall never know. He wouldn't *listen* to me, Nicholas!"

"Nor would I," said Nicholas uncomfortably.

"Yes, you would, darling. Only every time you said something so nice about your father that I couldn't go on. Your uncle wouldn't *listen*."

Well, let that be a warning to us, thought Nicholas. He did not feel very strongly about the matter. He agreed that Professor Pounce should be made to pay, although unwittingly, for his unfeeling heart. But he had a bad moment when he went downstairs and encountered his uncle in the hall.

5

"How's your mother?" asked Professor Pounce.

"She's packing," answered Nicholas. "She wants to leave to-morrow."

The Professor looked troubled.

"It was a curious thing," he said. "A very curious thing indeed. As you know, I witnessed her marriage myself."

"I know, sir."

"And I am morally certain that she has never—er—slipped up since. Never."

"I'm sure she hasn't, sir."

"If it hadn't been for that one incident I could have presented a most convincing body of evidence. If only your mother—"

"Couldn't you leave her out altogether?"

Professor Pounce shook his head.

"My conscience would not permit it. I must accept the facts without casuistry as without complaint."

For a moment Nicholas wavered. If only he could tell his uncle the truth under a vow of silence! But no such oath, he knew, would bind the Professor. His conscience might be scientifically strict, it was also, in the interests of science, peculiarly elastic. Professor Pounce would have not the slightest hesitation in laying the whole history of his brother and Miss Lovell before the assembled folklorists of the United Kingdom.

"I'm sorry, Uncle Isaac," said Nicholas feelingly.

"It's not your fault, my boy. You say your mother is packing?"

"She wants to leave in the morning, sir."

"Natural enough," sighed the Professor. "And you?"

"I think I'd better go along with her."

"We'll all go," said Professor Pounce. "You and I and your mother and Carmen. Our usefulness here is over."

To Nicholas that seemed an odd way of putting it, but he felt too sympathetic towards his uncle to disillusion him.

"We must tell Mrs. Leatherwright," added the Professor. He paused. "Do you know, Nicholas, that's a very mysterious woman. Here we've been living at closer quarters with her than with any one in the village, and we know almost least about her."

"She doesn't like being bothered," said Nicholas.

"Few cooks do. But her reserve is really exceptional. I wonder—"

"Uncle Isaac!"

"Blodgett-Blodger," muttered the Professor. "A strapping fair wench—Mrs. Leatherwright too is on a large scale—"

"Uncle Isaac!" cried Nicholas. "Stop! It's all over!"

"So it is," agreed the Professor sadly. "As you say, it's all over. An end has been made. But I do *wonder* . . ."

6

Strangely enough, at this last minute, with this last wild shot in the dark, Professor Pounce had hit upon the truth. Mrs. Leatherwright was the great granddaughter of Susannah Blodgett, who in 1805 migrated from Gillenham to Ipswich, and there set up as a laundress. She took her two-year-old son Enoch with her, and in due course apprenticed him to a French hairdresser named Duval. Enoch Blodgett, industrious and astute, eventually married his master's daughter, succeeded to the business, and for obvious reasons assumed the trade name. His daughter, Hannah Duval, was born in 1840, and in 1865 married Phineas Conybeare, a solicitor's clerk. Letitia Conybeare, the last of a long family, married in 1900 John Leatherwright, grazier, who died soon after, leaving his widow in poor circumstances. Mrs. Leatherwright was forced to go out as cook-housekeeper; but she was a good cook, she prospered, and the firm of solicitors who had employed old Phineas kept a friendly eye on her. It was they who had the letting of the Old Manor; and it was through them that Mrs. Leatherwright finally obtained her present situation in the household of Professor Pounce.

How much of this did Mrs. Leatherwright know? Enough to make the Professor's mouth water. She knew that her mother had been a Duval, but that her grandfather was not French. (She had actually seen him, on his deathbed in 1885, when her infant head had been thrust under his chilly hand for a blessing. She had actually seen the son of Susannah Blodgett!) She had also seen his bond of apprenticeship, kept in the family as a curiosity until her mother, Mrs. Conybeare, destroyed it out of snobbishness. On that bond appeared the name Blodgett, and Mrs. Leatherwright remembered it perfectly well.

She had remembered it and held her tongue. She was a woman of remarkable strength of character. She was also a woman who didn't like to be bothered.

Chapter 20

1

As night fell there brooded over the whole village a spirit of secret female merriment. For once, in that rural community, the women were on top. They had all that day received, so to speak, certificates of virtue, and the wives moved complacently under the eyes of their husbands, and the maidens wore an irritating air of untouchableness. The men, gathered at The Grapes, or in the village street, grinned tolerantly among themselves, but spoke never a word of disbelief—for no man could so speak without impugning the chastity of his own wife or sweetheart, which male pride naturally forbade. Thus the virtue of the women of Gillenham was an established fact, and the women were making the most of it.

"It's an extraordinary thing," said the Vicar to Mrs. Crowner, "but I've just had notice of four sets of banns. I never remember having so many at once before."

"Good heavens!" cried Mrs. Crowner. She knew from experience the tendency of the Gillenham male to jib at this decisive step; it could be put off, without real scandal, till the baby was three months on the way. "Good heavens!" repeated Mrs. Crowner. "I hadn't noticed any—any *signs*. . . . Who are they for?"

"Jack Uffley and Violet Brain, that girl Sally and young Fletcher, Mrs. Fox's Joe and Grace from Ipswich, and a pair of Thirkettles."

"What on earth do you think has come over them?"

The Vicar smiled regretfully.

"I wish you hadn't dragged me to Ipswich, my dear. I hear to-day's ceremony was a great success."

"You don't mean that dreadful Stone of Chastity-thing!"

"I do. Morally speaking, the whole village has a clean bill of health—at any rate the female portion of it. I imagine these banns are a first and happy result."

Mrs. Crowner sat up.

"But, Charles—I *know* that some of those girls—"

"So do I," agreed the Vicar mildly. "So no doubt do they. But the power of self-deception is very great. To be officially re-endowed with one's chastity after one has lost it may well lead to a belief that it has never been lost at all. To act on such a belief can bring nothing but good."

"Good can't come out of evil," retorted Mrs. Crowner stubbornly.

"By their fruits ye shall know them," countered the Vicar. "We have always disagreed, my dear, as to the nature of Professor Pounce's activities. Personally I consider four sets of banns very fine fruit indeed."

His wife laid her hand affectionately on his arm. "But not of any of Mr. Pounce's doings, Charles!"

"Of whose, then?"

"Of yours, of course. Of your sermons!"

The Vicar sighed.

"I wish I could think so. And perhaps, in a way, I have prepared the ground. But you mustn't flatter me."

"I don't, Charles."

"And I wish you could feel a little more charitably towards Professor Pounce."

"I'll pray for him, if you like . . ."

"Dear me," said the Vicar briskly, "so will I. I'll tell him so. He doubtless considers prayer an interesting superstitious survival—and I'd like to give him pleasure somehow."

2

In the bar of The Grapes, Mrs. Jim finished her scrubbing as Jim came heavily and finally up the cellar steps. He came up, and took a good look at her.

"That's still your Sunday dress," he stated.

Mrs. Jim beamed.

"Fancy you noticing! Looks well, don't it?"

"It does so," said Jim.

"And I looked well in it this noon—didn't I, bor?"

"You did so," said Jim.

She came round the counter and stood close.

"Were you proud of me, bor?"

Jim nodded.

"Well, say it, then! Go on!"

"I was fair proud of my old woman. I reckon I was the proudest chap there. Will that do you?"

Mrs. Jim heaved a great sigh of content.

"It took a lot o' getting out, bor, but it'll do."

He put his big arm round her shoulders, dropped it, and smacked her tenderly on the behind. Mrs. Jim sighed again, this time with pure love.

"Did you shut the cellar trap, bor?"

"I did."

"Then put out the lights," said Mrs. Jim.

3

At Vander's Farm the Pyes ate their evening meal in silence. They had nothing to say to each other. Mrs. Pye sat moveless and grimly brooding; for once in her hard-fighting life she had lost a moral campaign.

The Pounce forces were withdrawing from Gillenham not in defeat, but victorious.

But they were withdrawing. All of them. The Professor, and his nephew, and Mrs. Pounce, and Carmen Smith.

And Carmen Smith.

Mrs. Pye looked at her husband darkly. Her anger against him was remote and almost impersonal—not so much the anger of a wife against a husband as the anger of the righteous against the sinner. He had sinned, and he would be punished, if not in this world, then in the next: most likely in the next, for any temporal misfortune, such as loss of property, would fall on her also, who did not deserve punishment. A violent death might meet the case; but no bailiff, and she would undoubtedly have to employ one for the farm, would be as effective as Pye himself, and Mrs. Pye felt that all things considered he had better be left on earth a while longer. "No dung like the master's foot," thought Mrs. Pye; and prudently refilled his plate.

The one idea that never occurred to her was that when Carmen went, he might go also; and indeed such a thought never occurred to her husband either. He was a busy man, with two thousand acres on his shoulders. He regretted Carmen's going, but at the same time acknowledged it to be opportune. Harvest was in sight, when he would need his sleep. He wouldn't forget her; she wouldn't forget him; but they had each their own way to go. They each had money to make.

Perhaps the most they had done for each other was just that: they had forgotten, in each other's company, the making of money.

Mr. Pye did not know why he suddenly remembered his grandmother. No two women could have been less alike. He searched his mind laboriously, for he was not used to examining his thoughts, to find the connection. It was something to do with a present. He had supported his grandmother to the end of her life, but then he could not for his own pride and standing have done less: it wasn't that. Then he remembered that one market-day, at Ipswich, he had bought her a pair of china poll-parrots—going cheap, they were, on account of one being damaged; and she took and turned them in her old hands, pleased as plums, and said, "What's these for?" And he said, "A bit o' pretty for you, Gran." And she said, "Tom, I b'lieve you'll be saved yet." And wasn't that a rum thing to remember after forty years?

Mr. Pye looked at his wife.

"Where's those china poll-parrots?" he asked.

Mrs. Pye stared.

"In the parlour. In the cupboard, where they belong."

"Then fetch 'em out," ordered Mr. Pye, "and set 'em on the mantel here. I want to keep 'em in mind."

4

Very late that night, when Gillenham was asleep, when the Vicarage was asleep, and Vander's, and The Grapes, Nicholas Pounce went out into the garden and stood a long time staring up at the Old Manor roof. Its great chimney reared up strong against the stars, its broad slopes brooded solidly over the earth. It made Nicholas feel very young, and for the first time in his life he did not mind.

You had to be young once. You had to find out. You couldn't learn everything at one go, even about women.

Nicholas thought of Bridget, of Carmen, of Mildred Hyatt. They came into his mind in that order—Day and Night and the British Museum. From his relationship with each of them he had acquired a scrap, a shred of understanding. Bridget had shown him the adorableness of the innocent soul, Carmen the clean beauty of the flesh, and Mildred—

Nicholas remembered *Gone With the Wind* on the sofa, and for the first time saw the episode as funny. He laughed aloud. He laughed at himself; and at that moment, as he stood there laughing, feeling so very young, his extreme youth ended. His laughter had cracked the shell.

His thoughts turned to his father; the laughter ceased, but he still grinned. Sober, upright, industrious bigamist! Virtuous, immaculate Ephraim, so quietly getting away with it! "By Gum!" thought Nicholas. "I wish you were here now!" He stared up at the sky, and called to his father's ghost—the phantom he had so long been dodging, and for which he now felt such affection. "You don't think I mind, old man? You don't think I care, Dad, about being a bastard? I assure you," said Nicholas, earnestly addressing the Great Bear,

"I don't. And Mother'll get over it. I'll look after her." He paused: the intent to borrow a hundred pounds recurred: it looked rather shabby. "Tell you what, Dad," he said more soberly, "I'll try old Mostyn. Just for a bit. I'll have a stab at it. Anyway, I won't be sponging. Okay?"

The constellations, naturally enough, made no reply. The old roof, the old chimney, took no notice. The night wasn't interested in Nicholas. But Nicholas, emerging from his egg-shell, looked at the sky and the roof and the night and liked them all the same, and didn't feel injured that no star shot down to congratulate him on his new-found manhood. . . .

He took one last look, and then went in to bed; because to-morrow he was going to get up early.

Appendix

PROFESSOR Pounce's monograph on the Stone of Chastity was never (owing to the events recorded in Chapter 18) completed. He had gathered, however, some rather interesting preliminary material which it seems a pity to waste, and which is accordingly given below.

I. VIRGINITY—*Early Use of, for Catching Unicorns.*

> *Tantae est fortitudinis, ut nulla venantium virtute capiatur: sed, sicut asserunt qui naturas animalium scripserunt, virgo puella praeponitur, quae venienti sinum aperit; in quo ille omni ferocitate deposita caput ponit, sique soporatus velut inermis capitur.*

And the unicorn is so strong that he is not taken by the skill of hunters; but men who write of this kind of thing affirm that a maid (virgin) is placed in his way, and the unicorn comes and lays his head in her lap, and lays by all his fierceness, and so sleeps; when he is captured as though he were defenceless.

Tr. Professor Pounce, from Isidore
of Seville, Origines, Book XII, 2.
(7th Century.)

Note by Professor Pounce.

This is not exactly a test of Chastity, but it could obviously be used as such: though not in Anglo-Saxon communities, where it would be too repugnant to the sporting instinct. Indeed, the whole process, to any virgin fond of animals, must have been extremely distasteful.

II. THE STONE OF CHASTITY—*Modern Analogies.*

(α) *Chesterfield Steeple.* Permanently crooked (Personal observation, Professor Pounce) since the day it stooped to behold the entrance of a virgin bride.

Communicated by Mr. G—L— a commercial traveller, in conversation with Professor Pounce in the bar of the Old Grey Mare Hotel, Chesterfield.

(β) *Public Library, New York City.* The lions (stone) outside this building said to roar whenever a virgin passes by, but so far observed only to yawn.

Communicated by Mr. R— E— resident of New York, in conversation with Professor Pounce outside Buckingham Palace. Prepared to take his oath.

III. PHALLISM.

"Our Queen (Victoria) rules over, according to the latest census returns, some 100 millions of Pure-Phallic worshippers, that is three times the population of these islands, and if we merely say Phallo-Solar worshippers, then 200 millions."

MAJOR-GEN. FORLONG.

It is not quite clear why the Professor noted this. It must for some reason have struck him as interesting.

IV. COMMON KNOWLEDGE (GILLENHAM). *Source, Mr. Thirkettle, Senr.*

The following Chastity-table was made out by Mr. Thirkettle at the request of Professor Pounce. Mr. Thirkettle gave his reasons for the marking at the time, and at great length; but after the fiasco of the Trial, Professor Pounce feels justified in giving only the table itself.

	Marks
Brain, Mrs.	0
Brain, Martha	0
Brain, Violet	0
Fletcher, Mrs.	0
Fox, Mrs. Albert	0
Fox, Joy	0
Fox, Martha	0
Powley, Mrs. Jim	0
Thirkettle, Mrs. Ada	0
Thirkettle, Sally	0
Thirkettle, Sarah	100
Uffley, Grace	0
Uffley, Mrs. Noah	0
Uffley, Mrs. Tom	0

Mem. Chief cultural influence Mr. Thirkettle apparently moving-picture (circa 1916) *Last Days of Pompeii.*

The final entry in Professor Pounce's note-book was made the day after his return to London, and is simply:

FERRETS.

Probably no one will ever know exactly what was in the Professor's mind.

THE END

FURROWED MIDDLEBROW

FM1. *A Footman for the Peacock* (1940) .... RACHEL FERGUSON
FM2. *Evenfield* (1942) .... RACHEL FERGUSON
FM3. *A Harp in Lowndes Square* (1936) .... RACHEL FERGUSON
FM4. *A Chelsea Concerto* (1959) .... FRANCES FAVIELL
FM5. *The Dancing Bear* (1954) .... FRANCES FAVIELL
FM6. *A House on the Rhine* (1955) .... FRANCES FAVIELL
FM7. *Thalia* (1957) .... FRANCES FAVIELL
FM8. *The Fledgeling* (1958) .... FRANCES FAVIELL
FM9. *Bewildering Cares* (1940) .... WINIFRED PECK
FM10. *Tom Tiddler's Ground* (1941) .... URSULA ORANGE
FM11. *Begin Again* (1936) .... URSULA ORANGE
FM12. *Company in the Evening* (1944) .... URSULA ORANGE
FM13. *The Late Mrs. Prioleau* (1946) .... MONICA TINDALL
FM14. *Bramton Wick* (1952) .... ELIZABETH FAIR
FM15. *Landscape in Sunlight* (1953) .... ELIZABETH FAIR
FM16. *The Native Heath* (1954) .... ELIZABETH FAIR
FM17. *Seaview House* (1955) .... ELIZABETH FAIR
FM18. *A Winter Away* (1957) .... ELIZABETH FAIR
FM19. *The Mingham Air* (1960) .... ELIZABETH FAIR
FM20. *The Lark* (1922) .... E. NESBIT
FM21. *Smouldering Fire* (1935) .... D.E. STEVENSON
FM22. *Spring Magic* (1942) .... D.E. STEVENSON
FM23. *Mrs. Tim Carries On* (1941) .... D.E. STEVENSON
FM24. *Mrs. Tim Gets a Job* (1947) .... D.E. STEVENSON
FM25. *Mrs. Tim Flies Home* (1952) .... D.E. STEVENSON
FM26. *Alice* (1949) .... ELIZABETH ELIOT
FM27. *Henry* (1950) .... ELIZABETH ELIOT
FM28. *Mrs. Martell* (1953) .... ELIZABETH ELIOT
FM29. *Cecil* (1962) .... ELIZABETH ELIOT
FM30. *Nothing to Report* (1940) .... CAROLA OMAN
FM31. *Somewhere in England* (1943) .... CAROLA OMAN
FM32. *Spam Tomorrow* (1956) .... VERILY ANDERSON
FM33. *Peace, Perfect Peace* (1947) .... JOSEPHINE KAMM

FM34. *Beneath the Visiting Moon* (1940) .... ROMILLY CAVAN
FM35. *Table Two* (1942) .... MARJORIE WILENSKI
FM36. *The House Opposite* (1943) .... BARBARA NOBLE
FM37. *Miss Carter and the Ifrit* (1945) .... SUSAN ALICE KERBY
FM38. *Wine of Honour* (1945) .... BARBARA BEAUCHAMP
FM39. *A Game of Snakes and Ladders* (1938, 1955) .... DORIS LANGLEY MOORE
FM40. *Not at Home* (1948) .... DORIS LANGLEY MOORE
FM41. *All Done by Kindness* (1951) .... DORIS LANGLEY MOORE
FM42. *My Caravaggio Style* (1959) .... DORIS LANGLEY MOORE
FM43. *Vittoria Cottage* (1949) .... D.E. STEVENSON
FM44. *Music in the Hills* (1950) .... D.E. STEVENSON
FM45. *Winter and Rough Weather* (1951) ...... D.E. STEVENSON
FM46. *Fresh from the Country* (1960) .... MISS READ
FM47. *Miss Mole* (1930) .... E.H. YOUNG
FM48. *A House in the Country* (1957) .... RUTH ADAM
FM49. *Much Dithering* (1937) .... DOROTHY LAMBERT
FM50. *Miss Plum and Miss Penny* (1959) . DOROTHY EVELYN SMITH
FM51. *Village Story* (1951) .... CELIA BUCKMASTER
FM52. *Family Ties* (1952) .... CELIA BUCKMASTER
FM53. *Rhododendron Pie* (1930) .... MARGERY SHARP
FM54. *Fanfare for Tin Trumpets* (1932) .... MARGERY SHARP
FM55. *Four Gardens* (1935) .... MARGERY SHARP
FM56. *Harlequin House* (1939) .... MARGERY SHARP
FM57. *The Stone of Chastity* (1940) .... MARGERY SHARP
FM58. *The Foolish Gentlewoman* (1948) .... MARGERY SHARP
FM59. *The Swiss Summer* (1951) .... STELLA GIBBONS
FM60. *A Pink Front Door* (1959) .... STELLA GIBBONS
FM61. *The Weather at Tregulla* (1962) .... STELLA GIBBONS
FM62. *The Snow-Woman* (1969) .... STELLA GIBBONS
FM63. *The Woods in Winter* (1970) .... STELLA GIBBONS

CPSIA information can be obtained
at www.ICGtesting.com
Printed in the USA
LVHW032132170221
679356LV00003B/583